Mercenaries
A Mercenaries Bad Boy Romance
Anne Kane

Mercenaries
A Mercenaries Bad Boy Romance
Anne Kane

ISBN: 978-1-60521-948-6

Publisher:
Changeling Press LLC
315 N. Centre St.
Martinsburg, WV 25404
ChangelingPress.com

Printed in the U.S.A.

Editor: Crystal Esau
Cover Artist: Bryan Keller

The individual stories in this anthology have been previously released in E-Book format.

Table of Contents

Private Skirmish (Mercenaries 1)
Anne Kane

What do you do when the woman you love is up for auction? Make sure you're the highest bidder!

When her little sister disappears, Dee vows to find her. She follows a lead to Loden Province but is picked up by government troops and convicted of crossing provincial borders without a permit. The punishment? She is sent to be sold at auction.

As the auctioneer calls for bids, she hears a voice from her past. Kaeden! The lover she ran out on in order to raise her little sister. He's found her again, and he has no intention of letting her escape a second time. He and his band of mercenaries will do whatever it takes to reunite the sisters and keep them safe.

Chapter One

Dee glared at the guard as he nudged her back into place with the barrel of his plasma rifle. One lousy moment of inattention and here she was, waiting her turn on the auction block.

"Sold!" The auctioneer's voice rang loud as his gavel hit the podium and the dusky beauty from Uranus Prime was led to the holding cells on the far side of the room, a sultry smile curving her full lips.

"You're up, blondie. Smile pretty and you might fetch a decent owner." The young wrangler smirked as he grabbed the lead attached to the heavy collar around her neck. Dee followed quietly as he led her to the auction block, not because she wanted to be sold off like an animal but because she knew this wasn't the time to make a run for her freedom.

She glanced around. Too many guards. Too much security. The holding area was crawling with people of every description and not one would lift a hand to help her. She had been looking for her sister in one of the outer provinces when they arrested her. The penalty for leaving her home province without permission was indentured service for the remainder of her natural life.

When the Military Alliance ousted the democratic government of Earth, things had changed drastically for the inhabitants. The new rulers had lots of rules and little tolerance for those who didn't follow them. They found a creative way to get rid of citizens who didn't obey their every whim, without having to pay for expensive prisons. Sell them, and pocket the profit. Military efficiency at its finest.

Dee had every intention of escaping, but now was not the time. Maybe the wrangler had a point. A lax owner would make her eventual escape so much easier. If she played her cards right, she could be on her way by nightfall. She mustered up her sexiest smile and looked out over the room full of prospective buyers.

"What am I bid for this healthy young specimen?" The auctioneer beamed at her like a fond uncle. "Strayed into the wrong province and arrested without any damage to the merchandise. Turn around, sweetie, and let the crowd see what they're bidding on."

Dee gritted her teeth, keeping her eyes downcast to hide her initial reaction. Merchandise, indeed! She turned in a slow circle, ignoring the catcalls of a rowdy bunch of miners in the front row. They were just here for the show, they wouldn't have the credits to actually bid.

"Let's start at one thousand." The auctioneer launched into his well-practiced spiel, and Dee watched as the bidding became a contest between a jovial fellow with two dark beauties sitting quietly at his feet, and a rather nasty-looking man who smacked a riding crop against his boots every time someone bid against him. Lordy, if he won she'd have to make a break for it before he carted her off to whatever rock he'd crawled out from under.

"Come on, people. Look at her. New to the block. I'd bet my finest leather duster that she's never been used by more than one male at a time. Just think what fun you could have training her to your own tastes. Do I hear six thousand?"

"Six thousand, five hundred." The Nasty Guy's smile was as cold as an arctic outflow.

The Jovial Fellow hesitated a moment, and Dee's heart sank. She eyed up the exits, wondering which one was the quickest route to outside and freedom. There was no way she was going to let Nasty Guy take her anywhere.

"Ten thousand."

Dee's head jerked up at the sound of that familiar voice, her heart rate soaring. Kaeden! Where was he? And what the hell was he doing at a slave auction? He hated the government-run auctions with a passion that bordered on obsession. The only time he'd ever attended one was to start a riot and watch the slaves bolt for freedom.

Nasty Guy stood, his crop whistling through the air in agitation, and for a moment Dee thought he was going to bid higher. Her breath caught in her throat. He glared at the back of the room before spinning on his heel and stalking out of the hall.

Dee let out a relieved breath, her eyes scanning the crowd until she found him. Kaeden. The only man who'd ever managed to break through the wall of ice she kept around her heart. He stared straight at her, the hard glint in his eye telling her he hadn't forgiven her for walking out on him.

"Ten thousand! Now that's more like it. Anyone want to go ten one hundred?" The auctioneer paused, his gavel held in midair and a happy grin on his face. His cut of the sale price would keep him in black market ale for the next few moon cycles. "No? Going once? Going twice. Sold, to the gentleman in row nine!" The gavel hit the podium with a decisive thump, and Dee gave a sigh of relief. Kaeden might be pissed at her, but at least she didn't have to worry about being a slave.

He and his band of mercenaries went out of their way to disrupt the slave trade. He'd read her the riot act first, but he'd sign her freedom papers and she could be on her way. Next time, she'd check for government forces before she waltzed into a bar on the wrong side of a provincial border. If she hadn't been so intent on finding Wren, she might have noticed the captain's bars on the man's shoulder and avoided this whole unfortunate incident.

The wrangler led her off the block and over to the holding pens. Before he managed to shove her into one of the iron holding cells, Kaeden materialized at her side, his hand held out for the lead. "No need for that. I'll take her from here."

Dee watched the wrangler open his mouth to protest. There were forms to fill out, money to change hands and receipts to be issued. It didn't surprise her that after one look at the mercenary's hard face, the wrangler closed his mouth and handed over the lead without protest.

"You can collect the paperwork over there." He pointed to the harried-looking secretary and made a quick escape. Dee didn't blame him.

She looked into the chilly eyes of her former lover. He had aged in the time she'd been gone. The harsh angles of his face were more pronounced. She still found him absolutely irresistible. "You here specifically for me, or just slumming?" No point in letting him know how quickly her heart rate soared when she'd heard his voice in the crowd.

He turned those beautiful blue eyes on her and actually growled. "Shut up. You have no idea how angry I am right now. I'll deal with you once the paperwork is in order."

"Yes, sir!" The snappy phrase was out before she had time to think, and she winced inwardly. Now was probably not a good time to annoy Kaeden any more than he already was. She snuck a glance from under her lashes. Was that a sparkle of amusement she saw in his eyes? He'd always said her smart mouth was one of the things he enjoyed the most about her. Maybe he wasn't as pissed as she thought. Or maybe he was just happy that she'd managed to pick a fight with someone other than him this time.

Kaeden filled out the paperwork in his usual indecipherable script and handed over his cred-card. In short order they were free to go. Amazing how accommodating people got when the burly mercenary glared at them. She'd been on the receiving end of that glare often enough to understand.

He kept his hand wrapped around the end of her leash as they navigated their way back to the parking lot. Why wasn't she surprised to find he'd brought the entire team with him? If there was one thing she loved about Kaeden it was his tenacity. Once he decided to do something, he made sure he had enough alternate plans to make it work. If he hadn't managed to buy her, he probably would have started a small war to get her out of there.

"If you'd leashed her up to start with, we could still be snuggled up in the bunker with our beer." Jackson, Kaeden's second-in-command, unwound himself from the tailgate of the Hummer, humor twinkling in his dark eyes.

"I love you too, Jackson. You drink too much as it is, which is why you sleep alone most of the time." Dee smiled fondly at the dark-skinned man. Jackson would move mountains if he thought anyone were going to hurt her. He treated her like an annoying little sister. All the guys did, but when things got tough they knew they could count on her to hold up her end of the fight.

Kaeden pulled a large knife out of his boot. "Hold still." Using the tip of the knife to pry, he broke the collar open and pulled it off her neck. Tossing it on the ground, he ground it into the pavement with the heel of his boot. "Get in the vehicle, and get it moving. This place leaves a sour taste in my mouth." Kaeden climbed into the Hummer, grasping Dee's wrist to pull her in beside him.

"Aye, Sarge." Jason Tremble, a.k.a. "Snake," dropped the vehicle into gear and pulled smoothly out of the lot. "Back to the bunker, or do we need to make a pit stop for food? The princess looks like she could use a good meal or two."

Dee felt heat stain her cheeks. She'd been so busy chasing down leads on her sister's disappearance these last few weeks, she'd been skipping meals. She hadn't realized that it was so obvious.

"We can feed her better at home base. Just get us there before I'm tempted to go back in there and start a riot. I hate these damn auctions." Kaeden's voice was gruff, and his fingers were still wrapped loosely around Dee's wrist.

She sighed, forcing herself to relax. This wasn't so bad. The team still thought of her as one of them. They were pretending nothing had changed. That she hadn't quietly snuck out one night and left them all behind.

* * *

"You haven't done a thing with this place since I left!" Dee turned in a complete circle, taking in the beige walls devoid of anything that might personalize the room. "Good grief. How hard would it be to hang a picture or two?"

"Why would I want to hang a picture?" Kaeden stripped off his shoulder holster and tossed it on the bed. Next came the knife strapped to the inside of his leg, and the gun snuggled into the back of his pants. That was Kaeden, a walking ammo dump.

She plopped herself down on his bed and crossed her legs while she watched him. Although she'd never admit it aloud, just the sight of him sent little curls of heat skittering through her veins. Six and a half feet of tightly muscled male with golden curls tied back with a strip of leather, he reminded her of a picture of the Norse Vikings she'd once seen in a museum. He was the natural leader of the group of mercenaries, and he took his position seriously. He'd been the sergeant of Zebra Company during the provincial wars, and when his side lost the war he'd organized a mercenary group out of the soldiers that had nowhere left to go.

The group had its own agenda, though, and only took on contracts that they felt were worth fighting for. They made enough to survive on, and not much else. Not the most lucrative way to run a company, but then, money didn't mean a lot to people who'd seen everything they believed in blown to bits. For a government who claimed its only agenda was to look after the people, it sure had a high body count.

Kaeden opened the gun locker, wiping each piece lovingly before storing it in its spot. The guy was anal about his weapons. After he'd closed the locker door, he turned his full attention on her. "So now do you want to tell me what in the hell you were doing getting arrested across the provincial border?"

That mild tone of voice didn't fool Dee one bit. He was pissed, and that just pissed her off. He had no right to question what she did, or why. She was a grown woman with her own credits. They had been lovers, but that was all. He had absolutely no rights over her. She tilted her head, her chin held defiantly high. "No. Now if you don't mind, just sign my freedom papers and I'll be on my way."

The curve of his lips didn't inspire confidence. Dee felt a tiny flutter of alarm, but chose to ignore it. This was Kaeden. No matter how angry he was, he'd never harm her. Besides enhancing his strength and reflexes, when he'd joined the military back before the ban on genetic research the lab doctors had enhanced his protective instincts. They mistakenly felt enhancing protective instincts would make the men better soldiers. What they hadn't realized was that those instincts could conflict with their orders, causing the soldiers to react in ways not appreciated by their superiors.

One step was all it took to bring him right up to her face. His hand moved so fast, she didn't see what was in it. The quiet snick of the lock was her first clue that he wasn't going to just let her walk away.

She jerked her head around, her image in the mirror confirming what she already knew. He'd placed a tracer collar on her. Much nicer than the one she'd worn at auction, the delicate gold filigree circled her throat without any visible clasp. Just because it was pretty, didn't mean she liked it. "Damn you! What the hell do you think you are doing?"

"Making sure I don't have to put so much effort into tracking you down the next time. Do you have any idea how hard it was to find you? The team was just about ready to consign me to a padded room when we finally got a line on your location." Kaeden crossed his arms and studied her. "I think it suits you."

Of all the asinine things he could do, this had to be at the top of the list. The man was about as civilized as a grizzly bear. He simply had no clue. "It's a tracer collar. It marks me as your property. You have no right to do this!"

"On the contrary, I have every right." A satisfied smile lit his rugged features. "I purchased you for quite an exorbitant amount of money, and I actually have all the paperwork to prove it. You need someone to look after you, and it might as well be me."

"The hell it will. I can look after myself, thank you very much." She stomped her foot on the floor.

One raised eyebrow showed what he thought of that statement. "Really? In that case, why did I find you on the auction block? I don't think you would have been happy if the other bidder had taken you home. He looked a tad too bloodthirsty to make a very good master."

"I didn't intend to let him take me home." She'd forgotten how much of an asshole Kaeden could be when he disagreed with her. "I would have escaped once I was off the block."

"Yeah. Good plan. I'm sure he would have been quite happy to look the other way." He dismissed her argument with a decisive snap of strong white teeth. "Doesn't matter. That collar stays on until I'm convinced you aren't going to take off again. Running seems to be your answer to everything."

"Oohh!" Anger goaded her into action, and she lifted her hand to slap that arrogant smirk off his face.

She hadn't counted on his enhanced reactions, and he easily caught her wrists before she could connect. Forcing her arms down to her sides, he lowered his head and seared a punishing kiss across her lips.

She shouldn't react. She shouldn't. The last thing she needed was to lose herself in his arms. Again. She knew from past experience just how easy that was.

She held herself rigid for a few precious seconds while his hard lips moved over hers, his tongue sliding along the seam to demand entrance. Desire raced through her system as she struggled not to respond. Damn him, he knew the effect he had on her.

"You can't force me." She bit the words out between clenched teeth.

"I won't have to." The supreme arrogance in that statement sent a new surge of anger washing through her. The worst part was, he was right and they both knew it.

She held out for an eternity while his arms moved up to crush her against his unyielding body. He slid his hands up under her shirt, and the feel of his callused palms on her skin had her melting against his hard body. It was so easy, almost inevitable. All the damn man had to do was touch her and she turned into a melting pool of lust. Damn him to hell and back!

She caught his lip between her teeth and bit down, hard. The coppery taste of blood filled her mouth, but Kaeden just laughed. Picking her up, he threw her onto the bed and followed her down to straddle her hips. Grasping her arms, he drew them up over her head.

His eyes gleamed darkly as he stared down at her, and Dee could feel the desire coiled tight in her belly. It didn't take long for lust to replace the anger and she rolled her hips, rubbing herself against the hard bulge in his pants.

"Damn, woman. Have you any idea of the hell you put me through?" Kaeden stripped off his shirt, tossing it to the floor as he reached for the fastening at the waistband of his pants. "If you ever even think about taking off like that again, I'm going to whip you within an inch of your life."

"Yeah, right." The hurt in his voice made her feel just the tiniest bit guilty for the way she'd run out on him. "Shut up and get those damn pants off."

"Yes, ma'am." He complied with laudable speed, the pants and Jockey shorts joining his shirt on the floor. "And now for you."

It was amazing how quickly he managed to remove her clothing without actually tearing it off. Within minutes, they were both fully naked, and she had to admit this was the one part of their tempestuous relationship that she'd really missed.

She gave herself up to the heat coursing through her veins as Kaeden bent his head and sucked one nipple into his mouth, grazing the sensitive bud with his teeth. His big hands moved over her body, mapping every inch, and he slid one down to cup her warm mound.

Dee let out a soft moan, arching against him, and he chuckled softly. "Good to know you missed me."

She ignored the comment, winding her fingers through his thick locks of hair. He had no idea how much she'd longed for his touch some nights, and she had no intention of telling him. The damn man was too cocky as it was.

He slipped one finger through the soft folds guarding her sex and scored it across her clit. Bolts of lust exploded across every nerve ending, sending coils of heat curling through her belly. She let out a wordless whimper, her fingers clenching and unclenching in his hair.

Kaeden lifted his head, his expression fiercely possessive as he gazed down at her. "You belong here. With me. Don't you ever forget that."

He plunged the finger deep inside her, and she lost all ability to think, to reason. Reason didn't matter, only feelings mattered; the feeling of his finger scraping along her inner walls, the heat racing through her and sending her libido soaring. She moved her hips in time to the plunging of his finger.

It had been too damn long and she hadn't lain with a man since she'd left him. In no time at all, she felt the orgasm bursting over her, washing away everything as her sex clamped down on his finger, and she buried her face in his shoulder to muffle her scream of fulfillment.

While the aftershocks still rippled through her, Kaeden lowered himself on top of her, his rigid shaft bumping eagerly at her damp entrance. "You. Are. Mine!" He seated himself balls-deep with one massive thrust of his hips.

Dee whimpered, unable to speak as yet another wave of sensual heat rolled through her. How had she ever thought she could live without him? Leaving him the first time had been hard. Leaving him again would tear her heart to shreds. She had to find Wren.

Kaeden braced his arms on either side of her head, pulling his cock almost all the way out of her, and then slamming it back in. A darkly wicked grin lit his rugged face as he settled in to shaft her with a steady rhythm. In and out. In and out. His massive shaft sent quivers of lust blasting through her with every movement.

She locked her heels behind his back, matching him thrust for thrust as she clung to him with every ounce of her being. She could feel another orgasm starting hard on the heels of the first, curling up from her toes. It washed over her with the strength of a tsunami, sweeping away everything and leaving behind an incredible feeling of fulfillment.

She let out an inarticulate scream, clinging to Kaeden as the world dissolved into a rainbow of incredible sensations. She could tell the exact moment he joined her, his thick seed spurting out in strong jets that bathed her pussy with heat.

They clung to each other for what seemed like an eternity, two people alone in a sea of sensual overload. They drifted back to reality at a snail's pace, still holding on to each other. Dee closed her eyes and snuggled closer to Kaeden. Tomorrow would be soon enough to deal with reality.

For tonight, at least, they were together.

Chapter Two

"I have a sister."

She wasn't sure who looked more stunned when she blurted that little piece of information out, her or the guys seated around the breakfast table. She had no idea why she'd suddenly decided to share. Wren had nothing to do with this world. Nothing at all. These men were cynical, world weary and emotionally exhausted by the horrors they'd experienced in the provincial wars. Wren was sunshine and light. She was naïve and innocent. And missing. Maybe it was time to ask for help.

The fact that Kaeden and his band of mercenaries had showed up to rescue her from the auction block indicated two things; they still considered her to be one of them, and they'd been keeping tabs on her since she left.

Six pairs of eyes regarded her with expressions ranging from surprise to shock. Snake jumped to his feet, knocking over his chair. "We had no idea. Did we leave your sister back there at the auction?" Snake stared at her intently.

"Don't be silly. Of course not." Dee shook her head, almost amused at the relief visible on the man's face.

"Then why did you suddenly feel the need to enlighten us about your family ties?" He looked miffed as he picked up the chair and sat back down.

"She's missing." Dee fingered the collar on her neck.

"Missing how? Where? For how long? And why did I not know you had a sister?" Kaeden reached for her hand and pulled it away from the collar.

"If I knew where she was, she wouldn't be missing." Dee rubbed the spot where the old collar had chafed, glaring at him. While she understood his reasoning, even conceded he had a valid point, she still didn't have to like the damn collar. "Wren is my younger sister, and up until my mother got herself killed in a food riot, I didn't even know she existed. I guess dear old mom didn't approve of me as a role model. When she kicked the bucket, though, I was the only person left to take care of Wren. The child welfare people dug through Mom's papers and found out I existed, but it took them months to track me down. I'm not sure who was more surprised to find out they had a sister, her or me."

Kaeden shook his head, a ghost of a smile curving his craggy lips. "Can't say you'd be my first choice to look after a little girl."

Dee raised her eyebrows, surprised at how much that hurt. She was just as capable of looking after a child as anyone in the room. "And who would be your first choice? Shotgun over there?" She nodded at the company's sharpshooter, lounging against the counter.

"Well, at least I wouldn't lose the little tyke." An easy smile lit up Shotgun's scarred face. "How little are we talking? You have a picture? We don't have a contract at the moment. Maybe we can help find her."

Dee rolled her eyes. "Yeah. Where do you think I would have put a picture when the cops grabbed me?"

Shotgun just settled back into his seat and grinned at her.

"He's not dumb enough to answer that." Kaeden reached into his pocket and produced a shiny metal bracelet. Before Dee had time to blink, he snapped it around her wrist. "What with the shock of seeing you again, I forgot to give you this last night."

"What's that for?" She fingered the delicate silver swirls. The pattern was intricately woven and she couldn't even see where the catch was. "It's beautiful." Just when she thought she understood the wily mercenary, he did something like this. The thing looked like it cost big bucks.

"Don't get all sentimental on me. It's a com-link bracelet. Now I won't have to lose any sleep wondering where the hell you've wandered off to. I can call and ask."

Snake snorted, a derisive grin on his face. "Old Kaeden here thinks if you had a chance, maybe you might have called his sorry ass sometime during the last couple of years."

Kaeden picked an apple out of the bowl on the table and lobbed the fruit at Snake's head, barely missing as the man plucked it out of the air just before it connected with his face. "You haven't learned any manners while she was gone. Sit down and shut up." He turned to Dee. "We all have com-links now. If we're separated we can keep in touch. No big deal. Yours looks like a piece of jewelry so no one is going to question it. The rest of us have them hidden in different places." He pointed to the shiny green stone in the center of the silver swirls. "That big gem is actually a liquid crystal. It can receive pictures or files from any of us. Another one of Jackson's handy little inventions."

"Okay, I guess it will be more useful than a real bracelet." She secretly wished he had surprised her with a real piece of jewelry.

She looked at the men lounging around the room. She'd missed them all, missed their ready humor and their fierce loyalty to each other. Jackson, with his knack for all things techy. Pete the pyro, who loved to make things blow up. Snake, who grew up in the bayou and could sneak up behind you so quietly you'd swear he was a ghost. Trace, with his ability to track anyone without tipping them off. And last but not least, Shotgun, the team's sharpshooter. Once Shotgun went after a target, it was only a matter of time before it had a neat hole through it. Kaeden was the nominal leader, but each man was an essential part of the team.

She felt a smile curve her lips for the first time since she'd realized Wren was gone. "So if you guys want to help look for my sister, I'd really appreciate it. I don't seem to be making much headway on my own."

"Might be fun to go looking for an innocent person for a change. Not a lot of them around these days." Jackson stood, stretching to his full six and a half feet. "Tell us a bit about the sister and how you managed to lose her." He pulled a tablet out of his pocket, his fingers poised expectantly over it as he waited for her to speak. If information was available anywhere in the Ethernet, Jackson could find it.

"Go ahead." Kaeden leaned back and stretched an arm along the back of her chair. "Jackson's been getting bored lately, and you know how obnoxious he can get when he's got nothing to do. Sic him on someone."

Dee nodded. "Her name is Wren, like the little bird. She just turned twenty last month and she's small, but wiry. She has blonde hair down to her ass, and she usually wears it in a ponytail. Says it gets in the way if she leaves it loose. I was tracking down a lead in the Loden Province when I got careless and the feds picked me up and sent me to auction."

She paused, watching as Jackson's fingers danced across the tablet. "We were in the market sector, bartering some of the herbs we raised for meat when she disappeared. Wren said she was going to see if she could find some stakes for the taller plants, and I didn't even see which way she went. They had to be pros to grab her from a public market like that."

The nightmare threatened to overwhelm her again. The bewilderment when she couldn't find Wren, then the dawning knowledge that something was really wrong. Her sister wasn't a toddler; she didn't just wander off and get lost. Dee had been coaching her on her fighting skills, but they'd left their weapons in the truck, and Wren was still much too trusting.

"Take it easy. You know the drill. Details count." Kaeden took the glass of water from Trace and handed it to her. "The grunts picked you up two provinces over. What kind of lead was it?"

Dee took a long sip on the water. "I heard about a gang abducting young women. Rumor has it they transport them across the provincial lines so they are harder to locate." She paused, unable to swallow the lump in her throat. "Then they just disappear."

"Your sister. What color are her eyes? Any tattoos or identifying marks?" Jackson was all business, and it helped her to pull herself together.

"Hazel eyes, and she has a tattoo on her left shoulder, a bird. A wren."

"Does she know how to fight?"

Dee frowned. "Not well. I've been teaching her but she's a lousy shot, and can't seem to get the hang of aiming."

"How about close quarters? Hand-to-hand stuff."

"She knows a bit. If she's not outclassed she can probably hold her own."

Jackson looked over her head at Kaeden. "Might have something, Sarge, but it's not pretty."

Kaeden withdrew his arm and reached for the tablet. "Never is. Let's see it." The rough sympathy in his voice failed to calm her.

Jackson handed the tablet over, and Kaeden didn't try to stop her from reading it over his shoulder. The display panned over an arena where two young women, dressed in skin-tight suits and some sort of harness, were sparring. The style seemed to be some variation of martial arts with a few back alley low blows sprinkled in. As they watched, the taller of the two women swept her opponent's feet out from under her, causing the other woman to plunge backward, her head smacking hard on the ground. She didn't move, and the victor stood over her, her hands held up in a victory salute and a vicious grin on her face.

Dee frowned. "That's disgusting! My sister would never do that."

"She might not have a choice. It's a fight block." Snake shook his head. "They snatch the girls from all over the provinces, give them a crash course in fighting, and then stick them in the arena until one of them isn't moving anymore. It's broadcast on private channels and a bunch of sickos bet on the outcome."

Jackson took the tablet back. "I didn't find your sister on the competitor list, but she could still be in training, or they could have given her a different name. Give me a minute." His brow furrowed as he worked, making him look like a grumpy giant. "There. I hacked into the arena feed and pulled up the intake records." He held the display up. "Any of these look familiar?"

Dee's stomach churned with dread as she scanned the faces on the tablet. Kaeden's hand on her back gave her small comfort. "Nope." She dragged her finger over the display and more pictures sprang onto the screen. "Oh my God! That's her!" The picture was grainy, and Wren lacked her usual cheerful smile but it was undoubtedly her. Dee jumped up. "Where is this place? How hard is it going to be to go get her out?"

"Hard enough. It's back across the provincial lines, which means we all need fake IDs." Kaeden took the tablet. "She looks okay for now, but we need to move fast."

"Then let's go, Sarge." Jackson got to his feet. "I'll get the Hummer decked out and meet you around front in fifteen."

"You heard the man." Kaeden slid a reassuring arm around Dee's shoulders. "We'll need flak gear and as much ammo as you can pack. These guys are nasty." He dropped a quick kiss on Dee's forehead before turning her loose. "You too, darling. Your gear's in my room where you left it."

He turned to address the rest of the guys. "Let's lock and load!"

* * *

"Is this really necessary? I feel like I'm naked, and that's not very reassuring when we're heading out on a mission." Dee frowned at her reflection in the mirror.

Kaeden felt the corner of his mouth twitch with the effort not to grin as he admired the way the synthetic material clung to her slender form. She was right. The tight material made her slender figure look even more tempting than if she were totally unclothed. There was something to be said about leaving a little bit to the imagination. Right now he could imagine how the soft mounds of her breasts would feel beneath his hands.

His cock swelled behind the restricting material of his jeans, and he gave an inward sigh. It felt like he'd been walking about with a massive hard-on ever since he'd seen her picture up on that auction site. It didn't matter how many times they'd had sex in the past week, he still wanted her with the unbridled enthusiasm of a teenager with his first crush.

Walking up behind her, he wrapped his arms around her waist and nuzzled the soft skin of her neck. "You know it is. These guys don't see women as anything other than entertainment or broodmares. If you want to come with us you have to look like you belong to the team, and I mean that literally. The target will underestimate you if you look like just another slave girl."

Dee sighed heavily, leaning back against him and causing his cock to jump eagerly. "I know. I just don't like it."

Kaeden nibbled the skin of her neck, just where it disappeared under the bright blue material. "You keep rubbing against me like that, I'll take this damn suit off myself."

Dee turned in the circle of his arms and ran one hand down his chest to the waistband of his pants. "You know it's going to take Jackson a bit of time to get the equipment on the Hummer tuned into the all province system. I bet we have enough time for me to take care of this pesky little problem for you." She fondled the growing lump through the tough material of his pants, and the curve of her lip was sheer seductive magic.

Kaeden raised his eyebrows. "Little problem? I hardly think that qualifies as little or a problem. I seem to recall you being quite happy with the results last night."

Dee grinned. "Perhaps I've underestimated the issue. Let's take a look." She quickly unzipped his pants, and squatted to skim them and his shorts down over his hips.

Kaeden groaned as his cock sprang free. The woman had no scruples, but damn that felt good!

Dee sank back on her knees, tracing a line down his aching shaft from the tip to the tangle of curls at the base. "You have no idea how much I've missed this."

He begged to differ. He couldn't begin to count the number of nights he'd tossed and turned, unable to sleep without her warm presence by his side. When he had managed to close his eyes, the nightmares had haunted him. Dreams of her being hurt, hunted, abused by the multitudes of monsters that haunted their post-apocalyptic world. Not knowing where she was had been pure torture. She was his whole world, even though he'd never admitted it to her, and he'd failed to keep her safely at his side.

He wasn't about to let that happen again. He would do whatever it took to make sure she stayed with him. If she needed to go rescue her sister, the team would make sure that happened. "You might have to take that suit off after all." He tugged the material down over her shoulders.

Without a word, Dee stood and shrugged out of the outfit with a sensual grace that sent his lust spiralling even higher. The soft smile that curved her lips let him know that she knew the effect the sight of her naked body had on him.

Dropping back to her knees, she gently cupped his balls, squeezing the sensitive sac gently. Tongues of liquid heat roared through him. He closed his eyes, winding his fingers in her long hair as waves of lust swept him up. Peeking up at him from under her lashes, Dee wrapped her lips around the head of his cock, her tongue tracing the slit in the center.

Passion flared between them, raw and hot. It had always been this way. Out of control. Flaring instantly at a glance, a touch. She slid her tongue along the bulging vein that ran the length of his cock, and then slid the head into her mouth and began to suck.

Kaeden growled low in his throat, not even trying to control his reactions as he rocked his hips, fucking her face while she worked her way up and down his stiff shaft. This is what mattered. Him. Her. Them.

"Stop. I want to feel your tight pussy wrapped around my cock when I come." He gently pulled her to her feet and grasped her hips, lifting her up high before lowering her slowly onto his cock.

Dee locked her heels behind him, her arms wrapped around his neck. Kaeden used his amazing strength to slide her up and down on his shaft. Desire ricocheted back and forth between them. All the trappings of civilization dropped away as they lost themselves in the primal urge to join together, to become one.

He felt his balls draw up tight, his seed gathering before it exploded out of his cock in hot jets. He let out a roar of triumph as the walls of her pussy clamped down hard, milking every last drop of cum from his throbbing cock as her orgasm took her. Kaeden sank to his knees, still holding her tight against him. He was never going to let her go again.

"So." Dee's eyes shone softly in the artificial light, reflecting her satisfaction. "Do you think Jackson has that Hummer ready to go yet?"

Chapter Three

"Papers, please."

The border guard looked much too alert for Kaeden's comfort. Usually they barely looked at the paperwork before waving the team through.

Jackson reached into the glovebox and grabbed the forged documents they'd picked up on their way to the border, handing them over. The guard took it wordlessly, peered into the vehicle to compare each travel pass with the person pictured on it.

His gaze lingered a moment longer than necessary on Dee, and Kaeden had to make a conscious effort to relax. It didn't mean anything. With the skin-tight suit and a training harness on, she was breathtaking. Of course any male who could still breathe would take a second look.

"Are you going to put her in the arena? Be a shame to mess up that pretty face. Where's her documents?"

"Right here." Kaeden handed over the bill of sale he'd received from the auction house. No need for a forgery on that one. "She's not ready to fight yet, but I figured it would do her some good to see a few rounds. Kind of get her psyched up for it."

The guard looked doubtful. "You ever been to a live bout before? It's more likely to scare her to death."

The men all shook their heads.

"You might change your mind when you see one. I can think of a whole lot of more fun things to do with a pretty bitch like yours than have her beaten senseless in the ring."

Jackson flicked a look at him, but Kaeden kept quiet. While he utterly agreed, it wouldn't do their cover any good to let the guard know that.

"Okay, you can go. Enjoy your stay." The guard stepped back to let the Hummer proceed. Jackson quickly put the big vehicle in gear and pulled out of the checkpoint.

"Well, that went well. Now all we need to do is find the compound and look like a bunch of deranged lunatics who want to see a couple of girls try to kill each other." Snake grinned. "You guys shouldn't have a problem but I'm going to have to be careful."

Trace cuffed him across the back of the head. "You do deranged lunatic better than any of us. Dee, you might want to stay away from him."

"Hey!" Snake held up his hands. "I'm innocent! I wouldn't harm a fly!"

"Tell that to the guy you iced in Denver." Trace snorted. "Oh wait, you can't. He's dead."

Snake shrugged. "I consider that a mercy killing. The man was scum, and the world is a better place without him."

"True. But that doesn't make you innocent."

Kaeden interrupted the friendly banter. "Knock it off. We all know Snake's a warm and fuzzy kind of guy. Everyone clear on the plan?"

A chorus of yeses ensued.

"Good. Get your weapons on before we get there. Don't want anyone to realize we're armed to the teeth, now do we."

Dee turned her head, a frown marring the clean lines of her brow. "I'm not sure I can hide much in this suit."

"There's a wire down the inside leg." Kaeden pulled the deadly garrote out to show her. "And there's a pocket for a small pistol in the back of the neck. Your hair will hide the bulge, even in a braid.

Those are for emergencies only. I want you glued to my side the entire time we're in there. Understand?"

She gave him a saucy salute that told him she understood more than he wanted her to. "Yes, sir. Anything you say."

Shotgun let out a hoot of laughter. "That sounded kind of sarcastic, Sarge. Maybe you should discipline her."

Dee smiled sweetly at the hulking sharpshooter and made an anatomically impossible suggestion about what he liked to do in his spare time.

"I don't think she likes you, Shotgun." Jackson swung the Hummer around a rock in the road. "And we all know how nasty Dee can be when she doesn't like a person. You might want to play nice."

"Ahh. She knows I'm only kidding, don't you, darling?"

Kaeden listened to the team banter back and forth. For the first time in a long time, it felt good to be heading out on a mission. With Dee at his side, his attention was no longer divided. The team had been together long enough to feel comfortable letting each other guard their backs, and in the world of mercenaries, that was huge. Not many teams managed to stay together this long.

"Cut the crap." He pointed to a building in the distance. "That looks like our goal. Remember. We go in, locate Wren and get out. Period. No heroics. No starting riots because you don't like what you see. Keep in character." He felt his lips twist in a wry smile. Their cover was simple. A bunch of guys who liked fighting and females. Not much of a stretch.

The Hummer grew quiet as each of the team members checked their weapons and gear. Dee fingered her bracelet, the only outward sign of her nervousness.

As they drew closer to their objective, Kaeden could see armed guards patrolling the upper levels of the compound walls, rifles slung over their shoulders. Good thing they hadn't decided on a military approach.

Jackson slowed the Hummer to a crawl as they joined a long line of vehicles. Their intelligence had informed them a series of matches were scheduled for later today and higher than usual attendance was expected. So far, so good. They could lose themselves in the crowd.

A guard stopped each vehicle before allowing it to proceed through the massive wrought iron gates. As the line crept forward the team got louder, speculating on the day's entertainment. Dee kept quiet -- a slave girl wouldn't join in the conversation. When they reached the gate, a burly guard with an unkempt beard gave them a cursory look-over before motioning them inside without a question. They were in!

"Now to find the perfect parking spot." Jackson manoeuvred the Hummer through the maze of parked cars. "Close enough to the doors to be handy if we leave in a hurry, but with a clear line to the exits." He gunned the engine and squeezed between two Jeeps to claim a space on the edge of a line of vehicles. He nodded in satisfaction. "Perfect."

The team poured out of the vehicle. Kaeden looked around, committing the exits to memory. If things went south they would have seconds to come up with an exit plan. Wrapping the end of Dee's leash around his hand, he motioned the group forward.

* * *

The main arena was built along the lines of an old Roman coliseum, with a large fighting area ringed by rows of tiered seating. A festival air prevailed with loud men everywhere, and booths around the perimeter serving alcohol to their customers. A smattering of females were scattered through the crowd, but the majority present were male. Not surprising.

Kaeden assessed the situation. "I think we need to stay together for now. Jackson, can you tell where the females are held?"

"Just accessing the main grid now." Jackson's eyes had that unfocused look that let them know he was using his computer implants to access the information. "Okay, follow me. They keep the girls in a housing complex down below. Normally it's off-limits to guests, but today they've decided to let the crowds down to see the girls. That puts a kibosh on sneaking in and spiriting Wren out while everyone is focused on the fights. We're going to have to play this one by ear."

The team melted into the crowd, following the flow of people heading down to see the women. Kaeden could feel the tension emanating from Dee. He wrapped a hand around her wrist, and she looked up, startled. A brief, wistful smile flittered across her face. He wished he could do more to make her feel better, but they had to uphold the illusion of a master-slave relationship.

* * *

When they arrived in the housing area, they hit their first snag. The girls slated to fight that day were in a glass-enclosed pen close to the front. A video screen scrolled through their statistics with a constantly changing display of the odds as the betting got underway. It looked like a tall blonde with the build of a Nordic bodybuilder was the favourite.

Jackson shook his head. "There are four different holding areas for the rest of the girls, and I can't find anything that tells me where Wren is. We're going to have to split up to cover them all."

Kaeden hadn't liked the idea, but with this big an area and a limited amount of time there weren't a lot of alternatives. Three corridors led off to the housing areas. Security would sweep through the holding area just before the first match and clear everyone out. That gave them fifteen minutes to find Wren and get her out of here.

"Snake and Pete, take the west corridor. Shotgun, you and Trace take the one in the middle, and Dee and I will take the southern area. Jackson, you stay here and keep a lookout for trouble." Kaeden glanced around. "Any questions?"

The men shook their heads, drifting quietly away in the directions indicated. Kaeden stepped slightly in front of Dee and headed toward the south housing area.

Once they slipped into the south hallway, the noise of the boisterous crowd faded behind them. Kaeden ghosted his way down the passage, avoiding the security cameras with the ease of long practice. They came to the first of the cages, and Dee had to bite her lip. The cages reminded her of holding cells in a police precinct, with a toilet in one corner, a single cot for sleeping, and little else. Electronic locks secured the sliding doors at the front. The whole setup was highly illegal, but she'd bet her last dollar that the promoters paid off the government overseers to look the other way. Even after the collapse of civilization, greed still ruled.

They passed down the rows, searching for Wren without results. Dee glanced down at the timer on her bracelet. They had less than ten minutes left.

At the far end of the next row, a movement caught her eye. Instead of lying on the thin cot with a helpless expression on her face, a slender Asian girl was busy trying to short circuit the lock on her cage with water from the toilet. Dee caught Kaeden's arm and pointed.

He glanced at the girl, shrugging. "Not our problem."

Just then, her com link pulsed on her wrist, and a picture swirled into existence on the display gem.

"Is this your sister?" Trace's deep voice seemed loud in the stillness.

Dee stared at the display. Wren. They'd found her! "Yes! Is she okay?"

"A little thin but fine. Now how do we want to play this?"

Dee stared thoughtfully down the row at the Asian girl desperately trying to escape. "How about we let as many of the girls as we can loose, and then slip out in the ensuing pandemonium?"

A slow grin lit up Kaeden's rugged face. "I like it. Since we can do this quietly, let's make enough chaos that no one singles us out. Trace, can you two get Wren out of there and keep her safe?"

"No problem, Sarge. How are we going to get all the girls out of their cages? Jackson have some kind of tech magic up his sleeve?" Dee could hear the amusement in Trace's voice.

"Not this time. Use your pistols and blow the locks. Security will be looking for a gun-happy redneck, which pretty much describes the entire crowd here. If we're careful, we should be able to slip out without getting caught. Jackson, you got the collar and papers we brought to get Wren out of the province?"

"Aye, Sarge."

"Good. We'll rendezvous in the main housing area, and you get that collar on Wren. In all the confusion the guards won't realize you didn't come in with a female."

"Roger that."

"Pete? Snake? You copy?"

"Aye, Sarge."

"Then let's do it."

Kaeden pulled out his pistol and held it against the nearest lock. A dull popping sound echoed through the corridor as he blew the lock and moved on to the next one.

"Come on, girls! This is your chance. Make a run for it!" Dee watched as the women surged to their feet, calling to Kaeden to free them next. She pulled the pistol from its holster between her shoulder blades and jogged to the cage holding the Asian girl. "This might be a little faster. Stand back." She blew the lock and pulled the cage door open.

"No idea what you're doing here, but thanks." The girl gave her a brilliant smile before bolting down the corridor.

They worked quickly, each taking one side of the corridor and blowing lock after lock. Within minutes, they could hear the chaos starting back in the main area, and Kaeden gestured her to hurry. "We need to get out of here. Give your gun to one of the women and let's go."

Dee nodded, tossing the tiny pistol to a tall redhead. "The more of you that are free, the better your chances of getting out."

The girl nodded. "We aren't leaving any of our sisters behind. These assholes are going down!"

Kaeden grabbed Dee's hand and hustled her down the corridor. They emerged into the main holding area and skidded to a halt.

Chaos would be putting it mildly. The women didn't just want their freedom, they wanted revenge for all the pain and humiliation they'd suffered in those cells. The men who'd taught them how to fight each other were now on the receiving end of their skills.

Kaeden and Dee picked their way through the seething mass of bodies, ducking arms and legs. Thank God most of the crowd was unarmed or it would have been a bloodbath. Dee spied Jackson's head above the crowd, and she and Kaeden slowly worked their way in his direction.

By the time they managed to get to him, the rest of the team was there too, along with Wren. "Thank God you're okay!" Dee threw her arms around her sister, hugging her close. She had lost weight, but she was alive and here and they were going to be okay. That's all that really mattered.

"Hate to break up the family reunion and all, but we need to get out of here." Jackson produced a collar and reached toward Wren.

"Fuck you!" Wren broke away from Dee and used her forearm to block Jackson's reach. Then, she twirled to deliver a swift kick to his groin. "I am not wearing a slave collar ever again."

"No! He's one of the good guys." Dee winced. Apparently no one had explained what was going on to her feisty little sister.

Jackson slid out of reach, a wry smile on his face. "Suddenly I see the family resemblance. Someone want to explain to the little spitfire here what's going on?"

Dee slid between Jackson and her sister. "It's okay, Wren. In order to get across the border, we put these collars on and pretend to be meek little wimps. After we get back to home base, you can feel free to take a round out of any of the guys that don't treat you with respect, but for now you need to play along. They really are good guys. They came here for me, to help me find you."

Wren looked doubtful, but she took the collar and examined it carefully before snapping it around her neck. "Well, thanks for coming to get me, then." She gave Jackson a sheepish look. "And sorry about trying to castrate you."

"No problem." Jackson grinned, waggling his eyebrows at her. "I can use a new sparring partner. These guys are getting sloppy."

"I'll show you sloppy." Snake gave him a quick poke in the ribs.

Kaeden cleared his throat. "Maybe we could continue this after we're safely out of here? Jackson? Can you see an alternate exit? The one we came in might be a tad congested."

Jackson got that faraway look for a moment, and then nodded to the left. "There's a service corridor in that direction. It should bring us out at the trade entrance which is off to the side of where we entered."

"Lead the way." Kaeden pulled Dee in close to his side and pressed a small knife into her palm. "Just in case we get separated. You left your gun back there, and I don't think a garrote wire is going to be a big help in here."

"No, probably not." She tucked the knife up into the edge of her sleeve. Amazing how the little things let you know how much a guy cared. She resisted the urge to turn around and kiss him, giving his hand a quick squeeze instead. They were far from out of the woods yet.

"Wren, get in the middle and let's get moving. This is getting ugly a whole lot faster than I anticipated." Kaeden took the tail position, keeping Dee directly in front of him. Wren was in front of her and the rest of the team spread out loosely around them, with Jackson leading the way.

It was slow work pushing against the increasingly violent crowd but eventually they were in sight of the service doors. Jackson turned to check on the team, and a shadowy figure vaulted over the crowd and landed at his side.

It took Dee less than a second to recognize her. The Asian girl who'd been trying to escape. She flashed Dee a brilliant white smile. "You all look like you know where you're going, so I thought I'd tag along."

Jackson raised his eyebrows, his hand going to the hidden weapon strapped to his thigh, but Kaeden shook his head. "It's okay. Let her come. We can cut her loose when we get outside."

"Thanks. Name's Saralyn." She sidled up beside Wren. "So how's the little bird doing? You know these guys or are you just tagging along like me?"

Wren rolled her eyes and gestured at Dee. "That's my sister back there, and I get the feeling these are her playmates. No wonder she didn't want to introduce me to any of her friends."

Jackson used his pistol to blow the lock open and they all tumbled into the narrow service corridor. "Count six doors on your left, and the seventh should lead to the parking lot and our ride." He started down the long corridor at a quick jog, the rest of the team strung out behind him.

As they passed the second door, it swung open and a startled security guard stumbled into Trace.

Dee's breath caught in her throat. The big tracker dropped the unlucky guard with a swift chop to the side of the neck, hard enough to render him unconscious without doing any permanent damage. Dee and Kaeden stepped over the still body and kept going.

They made it to the seventh door without any further incident, and Jackson waited until they were all crowded close together before opening the door. Not unexpectedly, the parking lot was sheer pandemonium.

He turned, a huge grin on his face. "Only thirty yards to the Hummer, and I get to kick some ass on the way! Could life get any better?"

"Down, boy!" Kaeden looked stern, but the corner of his mouth twitched. "Do you have any idea how upset I'm going to get if my woman gets hurt? We need to get out of here in one piece!"

Dee knew she shouldn't be so happy to hear him call her "his woman," but she was.

Wren looked over and winked at her. "I don't think that man plans to let you run off to save me again."

"What are you talking about?" Dee avoided looking directly at Kaeden.

"I can do the math, and I bet the only reason you left a sweetie like Kaeden here was because you thought you needed to protect me." She rolled her eyes. "As if I haven't seen guys a whole lot worse."

"Sweetie!" Shotgun snorted with laughter. "And here we thought you were a tough sergeant. Sweetie!"

"I hate to break up the party." Jackson's dry voice was pitched low enough not to carry beyond the group. "But if we don't make a break for it soon the rest of the party is going to catch up with us and we'll never get out of here."

"Okay then." Kaeden became serious. "Jackson, you and Shotgun take point. The two girls stay in the middle. Pete and Snake take the sides, and Trace and I will bring up the rear. Any questions?"

"You want me in the middle with the other two?"

Kaeden sighed, addressing the petite Asian girl. "Don't you have somewhere else to go?"

Dee chuckled. "You unlocked her cage, and I think she's taken a liking to Shotgun. No accounting for taste."

"I certainly haven't taken a liking to any of you. I just know enough to throw my lot in with the strongest group."

"Ahh. I'm crushed." Shotgun turned the corners of his mouth down in a mock pout. "I really liked her."

"People? We need to move. Now!" Jackson eyed up a fight breaking out on the far side of the lot.

"Right. Let's go. Saralyn, you're in the middle with Wren and Dee."

"Thank you." She moved into place, and the group moved warily out of the safety of the doorway. Shotgun and Jackson strode forward, weapons in plain view.

"Are they always this protective?" Wren tucked an arm around her sister, ducking to avoid a beer can flying through the air.

"Yeah." Dee smiled softly. "They like to think we need them to look after us." Actually, after spending the last two years on her own looking after Wren, it was nice to have someone, or several someones, care about what happened to her.

"Close it up and move!" The tension in Kaeden's voice had instant results.

The team moved in on all sides, forming a tight ring around them as a clump of security guards appeared to the left. Damn. Those guys had really big guns!

Chapter Four

"You there! With the females! Stop right now!" The burly security guard didn't need a bullhorn to make himself heard.

"You suppose they mean us?" Dee felt a surge of adrenaline rushing through her. The rescue had gone almost too smoothly.

Jackson made a point of looking around as they continued to hustle toward the Hummer. "I don't see any other females, so yeah. He's probably talking to us."

"I said stop!" A loud bang heralded the warning shot that went whistling over their heads.

"Now that wasn't nice." Trace turned to aim at the leader with his snub-nosed pistol.

"Easy." Kaeden held up a warning hand. "We don't want to start a shooting war. Slow up a bit but keep heading toward the vehicle. Once they're close enough we can take them out without gunfire."

"Good plan." Jackson nodded, his hand dropping away from his weapon.

"But not nearly as much fun!" Shotgun shifted slightly to the left, blocking the guards' view of the women. "I bet I could knock his weapon out of his hand without even grazing him."

"And then the other four will start shooting. You know how bad those wanna-be-cops aim. They might hit one of you pretty boys and then what will you do?" Kaeden raised his eyebrows. "You can barely manage to get a date as it is."

Trace grinned, winking at Dee. "At least our dates don't flee four provinces over to get away from us."

Dee stuck her tongue out at the big tracker. "You have to have a date before you manage to scare her off."

"I bet your little sis here would go out with me. She said I was cute."

Dee laughed. "Good taste doesn't run in the family."

"I said you looked cute landing on your ass back there when the lock snapped." Wren joined in the banter as the group got closer to the Hummer and their freedom.

"Doesn't matter. I'm even cuter when I get spiffed up for a date." He ran his fingers through his hair and grinned. "So, dinner on Friday night? I know a great little place with live music."

Wren looked at Dee, wrinkling her nose. "Is he always this perky?"

Dee rolled her eyes, trying not to look worried as the security detail closed the distance between them. "He is kind of hard to take sometimes. You ought to see him first thing in the morning. Disgusting."

"A morning person, huh?"

"Yeah. And he power walks then, too."

"Really." Wren looked thoughtful. "We used to have a puppy that liked to walk in the morning. Remember, the little mutt with the floppy ears?"

Kaeden grinned, moving to the left to position himself between Dee and the security detail. "That's Trace all right. A hound dog if I ever saw one."

"They're trying to herd us." Jackson's voice was low enough not to carry. "Second group of bad guys at three o'clock."

"If we take out these guys, the new group will pull weapons." Kaeden's eyes narrowed. "We need to let them hit us at the same time."

"That's going to make it two to one." Snake spoke up. "Almost a fair fight."

"You're kidding, right?" Wren looked from one to the other.

"Nope." Kaeden shrugged, a lazy smile on his handsome face. "Three to one would make it even odds."

"Seriously." Dee nodded. "They may not look like much, but they're good."

"We don't look like much?" Kaeden wrapped one arm around her waist and pulled her to his side. Burying his face in her hair, he nuzzled her ear. "You looked happy enough to see me at the auction."

Despite the tension, Dee felt a familiar stirring deep in her belly. She strove to keep her voice light. "I didn't say Wren was the only one in the family with no taste, did I? Besides, I was just looking forward to a full meal. Those government types don't feed a girl enough to keep a bird alive."

"Little liar." He nibbled her earlobe. "Wait until I get you alone again. I'm going to make you beg, and you're going to enjoy every minute of it."

He let go of her and turned on his heel to face the approaching guards. "Everyone ready? Snake, Trace and Jackson? You take the group sneaking up behind us. Pete, Shotgun and I will deal with these yahoos."

"What about us?" Dee looked from one to the other. "We can fight too."

"Aw, that's sweet, darling, but I want to impress you with my manly attributes. Save your strength for later." Kaeden dropped a kiss on the tip of her nose. "You can watch, and maybe clap, if you feel the urge. Oooh and aaahh a bit. I like it when you do that."

"Glad to see you're taking this seriously." She'd forgotten how annoying he could be sometimes. She had a strong urge to slap that grin off his face. "Those guys do have guns, you know."

"And so do we." Kaeden patted the bulge at his waist, his face suddenly serious. "But that much noise is going to draw a lot of unwanted attention. Better we try it this way first."

He nodded toward the Hummer, one row over. "If things go south don't be afraid to use your weapon and get the three of you out of here. Fast. You've driven the Hummer before. Don't worry, we'll meet up with you back at home base."

Dee stared at him, taking in the sombre love shining from his eyes. He believed he was such a bad guy, beyond redemption after everything that had happened in the provincial wars. But she knew better. He had more caring, more commitment to what he felt was right, than any other man she'd ever met. He took responsibility for his team and believed that they could make a difference in the hellish mess their world had become.

She'd left him once, but she wasn't sure she'd have the strength to do it again. He truly cared about her, enough to do whatever it took to make her happy. He'd never even met Wren, but he made Dee's priorities his priorities so Wren became his problem too. They'd come for her sister, because he knew how much Wren meant to her. And for that, as much as she hated to admit it, hated the vulnerability that it brought with it, she was very much afraid she'd fallen in love with him.

A loud smacking sound behind her made them both jump and turn. The fight had begun, and Trace ducked as a uniformed guard swung a nightstick at his head.

"Be safe!" Kaeden gave her a quick peck on the cheek, and shoved her in the direction of the Hummer before turning to face the oncoming guards.

Dee watched as he waded into the group of guards, Pete and Shotgun on his heels. The three fought like one well-oiled machine, their backs to each other as they punched and kicked, using their forearms to block the guards' blows. They darted in under the guards' defences to deliver stinging attacks before retreating to the safety of their fellow mercenaries.

Sweat glistened on Kaeden's muscular forearms as he settled in to a smooth rhythm. Block. Kick. Punch. Repeat. Superior training soon began to show, and the guards began to make mistakes.

Mistakes were fatal in this kind of confrontation. The first to fall was their leader. Misjudging the distance between himself and Shotgun, he left his side vulnerable to a powerful chop to the neck that sent him crashing to the ground.

The sight of their leader lying motionless on the pavement demoralized the remainder of the group and they broke off the attack, fleeing toward the shelter of the buildings, but not before two more of their comrades were disabled. Dee felt a swell of pride as she watched the three mercenaries jog over to join their companions and rout the remainder of the guards.

The girls had managed to work their way over to the Hummer, but stood beside it where they had a good view of the fight. Wren gasped in alarm as Jackson took a hit to the side of the head. "Who are these guys, Dee? You never mentioned a band of mercenaries when you were living with me, but I get the feeling you know them real well."

Dee sighed, wincing as Kaeden's fist connected with a jawbone. "They're my family, as much as you are. I left them behind when I came to take care of you. I thought they weren't good enough for my baby sister, but they never stopped looking out for me." She slipped her arm around her little sister's waist. "Hindsight's twenty/twenty, but I think I should have just brought you to them instead of trying to take care of you myself. I'm not quite as tough as I thought I was."

"Oh, I don't know about that." Saralyn spoke up for the first time. "It took a lot of guts to come in here and rescue your sister. I don't know anyone who would be willing to put themselves in danger just for me."

"I wouldn't be too sure of that." Dee nodded at the men. "I saw the way Trace was watching you when we were working our way out of the building."

Wren nodded, giggling. "I think they call that lust at first sight. If you play your cards right, you could have that man wrapped around your little finger by the end of the day."

"Here they come." Dee had to restrain herself from running to make sure Kaeden was all right. "Let's get ready to roll." She yanked the door open and hauled herself up into the Hummer.

* * *

"You know I should spank your luscious ass for what you put me through the last couple of years." Kaeden ran his hand down the curve of Dee's butt, sending a curl of pure heat winging its way through her entire body.

"I know. I'm sorry." Dee placed her hands on Kaeden's chest, looking up at him with a contrite expression. "I should have told you about Wren right at the start."

Kaeden's eyebrows rose. "An apology? I think that's a first. Does this mean you're not going to take your sister and bolt as soon as my back is turned?" He picked her up and carried her to the bed, laying her down gently.

"No. I may be a slow learner, but I think it's pretty clear we're both safer with you and the team. Besides..." She pulled his head down to fasten her lips on his, letting her blossoming love show in the heat of her kiss. "I've been thinking it's about time someone did some decorating in here."

"You mean you want to hang pictures?" He lay down beside her, running his hands over her breasts.

She flipped him over on his back, throwing her leg over to straddle his hips. "More than that. I'm thinking fresh paint, maybe some nice trim. What do you think about installing some blinds to filter out the heat from the afternoon sun?"

Kaeden laughed, his hands resting lightly on her hips. "I can see the team is in for a major overhaul. You can do whatever you want, just promise me you'll never leave me again. I don't think I'd survive that more than once."

Dee leaned forward, the tips of her breasts brushing against his chest as she whispered in his ear. "Never. I've come to realize that I love you and hopefully you love me too. So, no more running and no more secrets."

Kaeden wrapped his big arms around her, pulling her down on top of him and squeezing her tight. "Of course I love you!"

"Well then, you'd better loosen up a bit, because I can't breathe!" Dee giggled at the apologetic look on his face as he loosened his grip.

"Sorry. I've waited so long; I never thought I'd hear you admit it." He ran his hands down her flat stomach, pausing to explore the soft hollow of her hips.

"I know. I was dumb enough to think I didn't need you, that what I felt was just lust. I missed you from the moment I left, but it wasn't until I heard your voice at the auction that I realized how much. The fact that you came after me and rescued me was kind of the clincher. That was a lot of money to pay for a girl who walked out on you without so much as a goodbye." She reached down and grasped his cock, sliding her hand from base to tip in one sensuous move.

"You know that money's going to come out of your decorating budget, right? Unless you manage to convince me you're worth it." The grin on Kaeden's face was pure mischievous lust.

"You mean like this?" Dee slid her hand up and down his massive shaft, pausing to fondle his balls. "Or more or like this?" Rising to her knees, she guided the tip of his cock through the soft folds guarding her pussy and settled back down, slowly impaling herself on the thick shaft.

"Oh, yeah. Like that!" Kaeden grasped her hips, urging her on as she rode him like a bucking horse, letting out little whimpers of satisfaction when his thick cock penetrated deep inside her time after time.

She felt the orgasm building, starting deep inside her and exploding out through every nerve ending into a thousand fiery fragments as Kaeden let out a growl of triumph. His seed jetted deep inside her, and she collapsed on top of him.

He wound his fingers through the curtain of her hair, claiming her lips. He kissed her with a passion that sent heat racing down her spine as wave after wave of aftershocks rippled through her. Cradling her face between his palms, he waited until she opened her eyes and looked straight at him.

Staring into her eyes, he declared, "You are the love of my life. Always. Forever. Don't ever forget that."

Dee sighed happily. "I won't. You see, I love you too."

Running Scared (Mercenaries 2)

Anne Kane

She's a genetic experiment that was never supposed to get out of the lab. If the government finds her they will kill her without hesitation. Her memories of her early life are sketchy but the one clear image she has is of a brother who saved her life, and then disappeared.

Jackson knows what it's like to lose your entire family in one bloody instant, and he vows to help Saralyn find hers. It doesn't hurt that he finds her irresistibly sexy or that the attraction is mutual. They enlist the rest of the mercenary team in a search operation that takes them into the heart of the corrupt government.

Chapter One

Saralyn ran her hands over the computer's input screen, sorting through the mess of icons with a speed that she knew suggested more than a passing acquaintance with technology.

There! She pulled the icon forward, tapping it gently to open its secrets. Closing her eyes, she splayed her fingers across the screen and let the information flow through the tips of her fingers, gigabytes of info flashing along the web of her nervous system to the storage cells in her brain. Later, she'd sort through the files and isolate the information she needed. Right now she just wanted to get out of here before...

"Looking for something?"

Damn! The overhead lights snapped on, and Saralyn turned to see the man they called Jackson lounging against the doorframe. Bad timing. Five more minutes and she would have been home free. One thing she'd learned at an early age was to hide her differences. Survival depended on blending into the crowd, not letting anyone know just how different she was. Just how much had he seen?

She plastered an innocent smile on her face. "Not really. Just couldn't sleep so I thought I'd see if I could find a game to play." She gestured at the bank of computers behind her. "I looked, but I can't find the game files. Maybe you can show me where they are?"

Jackson lifted one brow, a glimmer of humor shining in the depths of his dark eyes. He had nice eyes. Dark. Dreamy. Right now they seemed to see right through her, and she had to force herself not to squirm. Unfortunately that combination of bedroom eyes and the physique of a Greek god was making it hard for her to think.

Jackson pushed himself upright and sauntered into the room. "That's Trace's computer you were fondling, and frankly, I don't think Trace has ever played a game in his life. But you already knew that. I heard rumors about the government experiments, but I thought they terminated all of you years ago. How come you're still alive?"

My goodness, he was tall! Of course at five feet nothing, she was used to looking up at people. It didn't help that she was finding it harder to concentrate with every step he took toward her. She took a deep breath. "I have no idea what you're talking about. I've lived on the streets as long as I can remember. All the government has ever done for me is chase me away and make it hard to stay alive. And I was not fondling the computer!" At least not much. He obviously had an overactive imagination. "And how would I know anything about Trace's preferences? I thought all you geeky type guys were gamers. I've barely been here a week, and I'm still trying to sort you all out. Which one is Trace?"

He stopped right beside her, forcing her to tilt her neck backward to look up into his eyes. "Trace is our resident bloodhound. Tall, shaggy black hair, resembles a grouchy bear most days? Ring a bell? Set him onto something or someone and he'll follow the faintest of leads until he finally tracks them down. He can pull more info out of those computer banks than a buzzard pulls out of the garbage slews. I'm glad he's on our side, because he's one scary dude. I wonder what he'd find out if I sicced him onto you."

Saralyn did a mental tally of the men on Kaeden's team of mercenaries. Yes, she knew which one was Trace. That description was amazingly accurate. Then again, all of them were scary dudes, although she'd never admit that to them. Living on the run all these years had taught her that any sign of weakness would bring the predators swarming in for the kill. She highly doubted he would find anything of interest on her, though. Her life, for as long as she could remember, had consisted of an ongoing struggle to stay alive and find enough to eat. It was the second part of the statement that intrigued her. "So this Trace can find stuff? Or people?"

Jackson nodded, his eyes narrowing. "If anyone can find it, Trace can. Why? There something in particular you need to find?"

Saralyn opened her mouth, and was amazed to find herself telling the truth. Trust was a foreign concept and if a person knew what was important to her, they could use it against her. She had no reason to trust Jackson.

"Not something. Someone. I'm looking for my brother. At least, I think he's my brother." She sighed, her gaze fixed on the mosaic tiles on the floor. That sounded dumb. Explaining herself was another foreign concept, and yet with this man it felt right. "I don't remember a lot about my early childhood, but there's this one really vivid memory of me and him running away from some guys in uniform. I was real small, always have been. He hid me in a dumpster and ran the other way, leading the enforcers away from me. I'm not sure why but I know they were going to kill me if they found me. They were hollering that we stole something from them, but I don't remember what. Probably food." In this ravaged world, stealing from the government goons was punishable by immediate execution. "Anyway, that's the last time I saw him. He never came back for me and I've been on my own ever since. I realize there's a good chance he didn't survive, but I need to know. If he's alive and out there, I want to find him. He risked his own life to save mine. I can't let it go until I find out what happened that day. Somehow, I'm sure it's the key to a lot of weird things in my life."

There might be a hint of sympathy sparkling in the depths of the mercenary's dark eyes, but it was overshadowed by suspicion. He didn't believe her. For once in her life, she'd told the pure unadulterated truth, and he didn't believe her. That really stung.

Whatever! She didn't need him. She'd gotten this far on her own, and she'd finish on her own. She was so close. She'd find out what happened that day and she'd find her brother, if he were still alive. Tilting her head at a defiant angle, she swept past Jackson, heading for the door.

"Wait." Jackson caught her arm. "We can help. My team can help you find your brother."

"Why would you bother? You don't believe me." She spat out the accusation in cold tones.

Jackson shrugged, not looking in the least repentant. "I saw what you did with that computer and I tend to be somewhat cynical. Most mercenaries are. Hazard of the trade, but if you're serious about finding this brother of yours our charming little band is your best bet."

"I already have whatever was in that computer." She might as well admit to mining the data in their computer banks. He'd caught her in the act. "If your buddies have any information, I don't need you to give it to me."

Jackson shrugged. "Whatever you found on the computer is a mere pittance. Trace would have buried anything important behind more firewalls than you've ever seen."

What was it about this man? One look from those dark eyes and she found herself being honest with him when she hadn't realized she knew how. This close, his scent teased her nostrils, a musky male scent that sent heat racing through her body. It had been a long time since any man had been able to elicit a response from her. Sex was a commodity, a means to getting what she wanted.

Maybe it was just hormones. Sometimes her body had an annoying tendency to let her down. She inhaled slowly, trying to identify the reason his scent had such a huge effect on her.

A quizzical frown creased the mercenary's forehead. "Did I forget to shower or something?"

Saralyn could feel the heat stain her cheeks, and she bowed her head in embarrassment. This whole encounter was bizarre. "No. It's just... something about you." Why on earth had she said that? Time to get this conversation back on an impersonal footing. "You think Trace would be able to help me find my brother?"

"If anybody can find him, Trace can." There was absolute certainly in his voice. "You want me to go wake him now, or do you think you can wait until morning?"

He was kidding, right? He'd actually go wake this Trace guy up? "I've been searching for years. I think it can probably wait until morning. I should probably go try to get some sleep."

A hint of a smile curved Jackson's lips, and he gave her a conspiratorial wink. "Yeah. That grouchy bear thing gets worse if you try to wake him up. I'll call a team meeting after breakfast and you can tell them whatever you remember. We're a democratic bunch -- we vote on whether or not to take a mission. For what it's worth, I'll put in a good word for you. And I won't mention what I just saw. I like to see families get reunited, and it's rare in this godforsaken place. You should go try to get some sleep now. You look tired."

She got the feeling that he didn't smile often, and even now it didn't quite carry to his eyes. There was something sad lurking in the depths of those dark eyes, something almost haunted. It hit a chord hidden deep inside her. "I am, but sleep is hard to come by. Truth is, I could probably sleep forty-eight hours straight if I could just get my mind to stop running in circles."

Jackson nodded sympathetically. "Know the feeling well." Reaching out, he gently tucked an errant strand of hair behind her ear.

His fingers brushed her cheek, sending an electric spark of awareness sizzling across the surface of her skin. She'd never felt anything like it, had never reacted to a man's touch in such an intense way. She turned her face into the palm of his hand, sucking a deep breath into her lungs as she wordlessly asked for more.

Time slowed as Jackson lowered his head and brushed an achingly sweet kiss across her lips. Heat ignited deep within her, blazing to life at the instant of contact. Eyes closed, she savoured the sweet, sensual caress of his mouth as it moved across hers. He was incredibly gentle, barely touching her and yet she yearned for more. She wanted to wrap her arms around him and hold him close, meld her body with his, remove the clothing that kept them from joining, skin to skin.

What the hell? She'd never reacted to a man's touch like this. She was cool. Calm. Always in control. This man was a danger to everything she'd ever learned in the harsh world of the streets. There, letting

Anne Kane   Mercenaries

anyone get too close was dangerous, possibly fatal. And yet...

Jackson straightened up, his body withdrawing, leaving her feeling cold and bereft. She had to restrain herself from reaching out to pull him back to her.

"Sleep well, my little flower." Soft as a feather duster, his voice soothed her ragged nerves, calming her down as nothing else could. He turned, gliding out of the room in perfect silence, leaving her to stare at his retreating back in bewilderment.

What was it about this man?

* * *

Jackson forced himself to keep walking, not looking back. Saralyn touched him in a way no women had ever managed, thawing that corner of his heart that he thought he'd lost when his family had been massacred all those years ago.

Tomorrow, he'd gather the team and convince them to help her. Right now he needed to do some research of his own. When he'd first looked into the computer room, he could have sworn Saralyn was physically connected to the computer banks through the fingers she had splayed across the screen. Years ago, the government had conducted experiments on street orphans, turning the unfortunate waifs into human/computer hybrids who could do just that. The cybernetic beings had been incredibly talented, able to connect themselves to all types of electronic equipment with a mere touch. The government had been ecstatic at first, picturing a whole new step in man's evolution.

Their elation had been short-lived. The newly created cyborgs had proved too volatile to control. They turned on their handlers, refusing to be controlled. Their self-reliant attitudes caused panic and

- 58 -

pandemonium in the ranks of the enforcers who thrived on control. The project was terminated, along with all of the unfortunately enhanced orphans.

Although the government vehemently denied it, there were rumors that some of the children had escaped before the government goons could silence them permanently. The thought that the wraith-thin Asian girl they'd rescued from the arena holding pens could be one of the lost children both intrigued and terrified him.

* * *

Jackson took a cursory glance around the room. They were all here. His buddies. His teammates. All he had left that could be called his family. Now all he had to do was convince them to help the strange little Asian girl with the perpetual frown on her face find the brother she wasn't sure she had. And if his suspicions proved correct, put themselves directly in the crosshairs of a government cleaner team who'd been hunting her for the last decade. Not a thought conducive to a peaceful day.

He glanced over at Saralyn. She sat on an overstuffed chair in the corner of the room where she could see everybody while managing to keep herself almost hidden from them. Yeah, she'd been running scared for a long time. Probably as long as she could remember. The two sisters, Wren and Dee, were close by, keeping an eye on their new friend. If any of the team upset her, they'd have to deal with those two, and it wouldn't be pretty.

Trace lounged on a tall stool by the window. If you didn't know him you'd think he was daydreaming, his gaze focused on something outside. In reality he was taking everything in without allowing his reactions to show. Some habits are hard to break, and he'd spent a lot of time stonewalling government agents.

Shotgun and Snake sat at opposite ends of the sofa, tossing a practice grenade back and forth while calling out good-natured insults to each other. They looked like a couple of simpleminded rednecks, but Jackson knew that when it counted, they would instantly become a lethal combination.

Kaeden, the team's leader, leaned against the wall behind Dee, his arms crossed on his chest while his restless gaze kept track of the men. His team. Each of them had their own reason for becoming a mercenary, but to a man they were as loyal a bunch as one could want.

"There a reason for this get-together or did you just want to see our smiling faces?" Snake's lazy drawl cut across the idle chatter.

Jackson acknowledged him with a nod. "I could live another day without seeing your ugly mug. I have a proposition for the team."

A subtle shift in the men's stance showed they were paying attention. Jackson glanced over at Saralyn, giving her a reassuring smile. She'd been reluctant to ask for help, and he didn't blame her. Sometimes the team could be a bit intimidating to outsiders, and she'd been going it alone for a very long time.

"Our new little friend over there, Saralyn, needs our help. I'm going to let her lay it out for you, and I want you to pay real close attention because I've already decided to help her and I'd sure like to be able to count on all of you when I do." He motioned Saralyn forward. "Come on up here and tell us what you need us to do."

Jackson watched as Saralyn got to her feet in one graceful move. Her lithe body moved with a dancer's grace as she glided to the front of the room and turned to face the team. His cock swelled beneath the confining material of his jeans, and he silently cursed his traitorous body. A dalliance with Saralyn would be a bad idea. He barely knew this girl, and what he did know suggested that she wasn't entirely human. He'd watched her connect to a computer without the usual peripherals, and that could mean only one thing: cyborg. His instincts told him that she was telling the truth when she denied it, but that didn't make sense. Either she truly had no idea of what she was, or she was the most consummate liar he'd ever met. He wasn't sure which one he'd prefer.

Her eyes moved constantly, taking in every person, every movement in the room. Survival skills. They all had them, the little things that kept them alive. She was petite, and her Asian heritage gave her an exotic look that he found appealing.

"I am Saralyn, and as Jackson already told you, I would like your help." She glanced over at him. "I've been on my own pretty much forever. I have no memory of my parents, but I do have one memory of a brother. He helped me escape, saved my life, but then he disappeared. I want to find him."

He wanted to go and fold her in his arms and make all the hurt go away. He knew what it felt like to lose your whole family and he knew that he would move heaven and earth if he thought even one of his own family were still alive. He gave her a reassuring smile, nodding for her to go on.

"I've been working on this for a long time. I found a picture of him in a newsie feed a couple of years ago so I'm pretty sure he's still alive. I've been hacking the government comps in the different provinces, moving on every time I hit a dead end. Jackson seems to think that your people can help me."

"What's he look like, this brother of yours? Do you have a picture? Does he have any identifying marks? Tats? Scars?" Trace leaned forward, his face animated.

"Down, boy. We haven't agreed to take the case, yet." A wry smile curved Kaeden's lips. "Although I think our boy Jackson is going to be upset if we say no."

"Yeah, he's sweet on the little thing." Snake snorted. "I never thought I'd see the day Jackson would let a girl get under his skin."

Shotgun nodded, an exaggerated frown on his face. "Do you think she's a witch? Or maybe using some of that Far East voodoo stuff on him?"

Snake pretended to consider it. "Nah. I think she might have smiled at him. Maybe batted those long lashes. Girls do things like that, and poof. A man's senses desert him entirely."

"Okay, guys, enough." Jackson cuffed Snake lightly across the side of his head. "You need to hear the rest of this story. There's a little more to it that you need to know." He turned and nodded to Saralyn. She looked so calm and collected, standing in front of his team. He was proud of her and scared for her at the same time. She wanted to find her brother and that just might put her in the path of the men he suspected wanted her dead.

"I'm not sure why the men were chasing us. Jackson here has some kind of conspiracy theory going because he knows I have a few quirks that aren't normal." She threw him an irritated glance. "I doubt it. I don't remember but I'm sure those enforcers were chasing us for something normal like theft. We were orphans and we needed to eat. Other than that, there's not a lot to tell. I always seem to be running, but again, my lifestyle doesn't endear me to our government. They like people they can track and control."

Kaeden straightened up, a frown knitting his forehead. "What kind of quirks are we talking about?"

Saralyn glanced over at Jackson, fear clouding her beautiful eyes. He knew she didn't want to tell the team about her abilities but it was crucial that they knew everything before they formulated a plan. That they'd agree to help her was a given. He nodded, giving her what he hoped was a reassuring smile.

Saralyn sighed. "I have an affinity for electronics. I can touch a computer and know what's on the hard drive. My fingers let me connect somehow. Computers. Comm links. Security systems. If it's electronic and it has any kind of motherboard or microchip in it, I can hack it just by touching it. I don't know why, I just can."

The lost children.

The thought hung in the air as the tension in the room escalated to a whole new level, the jovial atmosphere vanishing in the blink of an eye.

Kaeden's eyes narrowed. "You have no memory of your early childhood? Parents? Family? Just a boy helping you to hide from a squad of enforcers?"

She nodded. "Not all that uncommon back then. Or now, for that matter." She sounded defensive.

"You must have heard the stories about the lost children. Did it ever occur to you that you might be one of those children?"

She stared at him as if he'd grown a second head. "Don't be ridiculous. You know those stories have been exaggerated beyond belief. Lab rat kids with super abilities? Sure, I can hack all kinds of information, but there's one tiny glitch that makes it so very not useful. You see, I can take the information out of the computers but then it's stuck inside my head. Besides, you know if even a fraction of what they say is true the government would never let those kids out of their sight. They certainly wouldn't have butchered them all."

"Jackson." Kaeden turned to face him. "Sounded to me like you know a thing or two that you might want to share with your buddies. What can our little princess here do that she shouldn't be able to?"

Jackson shrugged. Saralyn may consider her abilities to be quirks but there was no way she came by them naturally. The *lost children* fable was the only plausible explanation. "She told you the truth. I saw her mine info out of Trace's computer with a touch of her fingers. I believe she is one of the lost children, which brings up two very important questions."

"Which are?" Kaeden cocked one eyebrow

"Who is the person she thinks is her brother, and where is he now?"

"Well." A familiar grin creased Kaeden's rugged face. "I guess we're going to have to help her find the answers to those questions. Are you all in?"

Heads nodded around the room, and Jackson strode over to Saralyn, dropping his arm across her shoulders. "When this bunch decide to do something, it gets done. We'll find that brother of yours ASAP."

Chapter Two

"Are you sure we shouldn't be down there helping Trace?" Saralyn paced the width of the common room, feeling the tension in every muscle of her body. "What if he needs to know something and he can't find me to ask?"

Jackson chuckled, reaching out with one arm to pull her up against him. "Trace doesn't appreciate anyone distracting him while he's working, and just having you there would qualify as a distraction. He's actually very antisocial."

Saralyn considered breaking free of the circle of his arms. She opened her mouth, tilting her head back to tell him to keep his hands to himself but the look in his eyes made the words melt away unspoken. Pure sensual heat blazed from their depths, igniting a matching flame deep inside her. Combine that look with the arousing male scent rising from his hard body, and she had to make a real effort not to melt against him like some pathetic doxy from the local bar pool.

She pushed ineffectually against the iron band of his arms. "I promise I won't go upset your antisocial buddy, so you can let me go now."

A spark of humor curved the corner of his sensual lips. "Relax. I'm not going to bite you. Unless you want me to, of course. It's going to take Trace some time to get a line on your brother so we might as well kill the time exploring the spark between us."

Sunlight flooded through the window behind her, highlighting the rugged line of his jaw and the muscular line of his shoulders. Damn! Now that she was so close to solving the mystery of her past, the last thing she needed was some muscle-bound mercenary distracting her from her goal.

She fixed him with a steely look. "While I appreciate you letting me ask your team for help in finding my brother, that does not give you any kind of rights to my body. So, if you don't get your hands off me I'm going to have to hurt you."

Jackson stared at her in disbelief for a long second before he snorted out a laugh. "You're going to hurt me? That's cute."

Okay, that was the last straw. Drawing in a deep breath, she stomped down on his instep as hard as she could while giving him a sharp elbow to the diaphragm.

Unfortunately the whole thing would have gone better if he hadn't moved his foot at the last second and turned his body slightly so that the lethal elbow she'd intended to knock the breath out of him barely managed to make contact with the edge of his ribs.

"Not nice." His breath fanned across her cheek, warm and intimate. "You don't really want to fight me and you know it."

"I don't?" She kept her voice low, not wanting to attract the attention of the rest of the team. "What makes you think you have any idea about what I want?"

"I can feel your heart beating against me, the rhythm increasing every time I touch you. Your eyes are sparkling with desire, and I'm willing to bet your pussy is getting wet in anticipation. I don't have to be a rocket jockey to know that means you want to feel me buried deep inside you almost as much as I want to feel your hot sex closing tight around my cock."

He wanted her! The mental image that his words conjured up left her feeling breathless and needy. This was insane. Sex was a tool that she used to get what she wanted. She never let herself get emotionally involved, and yet she found herself wondering what Jackson's preferences were, and if she'd live up to his expectations.

Insanity!

It was hormones. That's all. She'd been celibate too long. She just needed to get laid and get him out of her system. Jackson was obviously willing. More than willing if that lump pressing into her belly was any indication. Reaching up, she wound her arms around his neck.

Jackson chucked softly. "Now that's more like it." Lowering his face, he skimmed a soft kiss across her parted lips. "How about we retire to my room? Much as I'd love to take you right here on the floor, I don't want the rest of the team wandering in and disturbing us."

It was her turn to chuckle. "Not into sharing? That's too bad. Your sarge looked like he could make a girl very happy."

"I'm sure he makes Dee very happy. And she returns the favour, so you're going to have to settle for just me. And no, I definitely don't like the idea of sharing one luscious square of your tender flesh with my teammates. They can damn well go find their own women."

Saralyn jumped as his hand came down on her buttocks, just hard enough to smart. He didn't want to share her. Now why did that send a hot thrill spiralling through her gut? "So where's this room of yours?"

"Not nearly as close as I'd like."

In the blink of an eye Saralyn found herself scooped up in Jackson's muscular arms. Striding out of the common room, he headed down a long hallway and kicked open a door on the left. He ducked to avoid hitting his head on the low doorway, crossing the room to toss her on an overstuffed bed against the far wall.

"Strip." He grunted out the single word, and then proceeded to follow his own order. Saralyn sucked in a long breath as he skimmed his pants down over his hips, uncovering his cock. Long and thick, it curved proudly upward. Oh yeah. She needed to get herself some of that.

Completely naked, Jackson pounced on the bed, straddling her. Flashing her a wide, sexy grin, he cupped her head in his hands. "So how come you still have clothes on?"

His enthusiasm was contagious, and Saralyn allowed herself to return the grin. It was just sex, after all. "The sight of your magnificent body had me so captivated I couldn't move." She batted her eyelashes in an exaggerated flirt.

"I can see how that could be a problem." Barely suppressed laughter sounded in his voice. "I have that effect on a lot of women. Don't worry though, I can help get you past it." Reaching down, he grasped the bottom of her shirt and pulled it up over her head before flicking the front clasp of her bra open. The lacy material sprang apart, allowing her breasts to spill free. Cool air feathered across the sensitive mounds, causing her nipples to form into hard-pebbled peaks.

"Gorgeous! Do you have any idea how exotically tempting you look?" Jackson's eyes darkened with desire. Lowering his head, he traced each dark circle with the tip of his tongue.

Saralyn gasped as shivers of pleasure washed through her. He was so large, so amazingly male. She felt incredibly open and vulnerable, her legs spread wide while she lay trapped beneath his superior weight with only the thickness of her jeans between him and her total surrender. She was operating purely on instinct, perfectly aware that it could lead to any number of undesirable results. And she didn't care. Reaching down, she unsnapped the closure on her jeans.

Jackson worked his way down her body, kissing and licking every available inch of bare flesh. She could feel the warm heat radiating from his bare skin as he worshipped her body with his mouth and hands. His tongue traced a line just above the waistband of her jeans, and he raised his head.

Saralyn's breath caught in her throat at the deeply sensual expression in his expressive eyes. Tension radiated in every line of his body, in the bold set of his face. Jackson was not some weak government official that she could manipulate with sex. She had a feeling that as a lover, he would be more addictive than any drug. The thought was intoxicating.

His eyes glittered as he pushed the denim down over her hips, leaving her covered in nothing but a scrap of lace that revealed more than it hid.

Saralyn moaned softly, her skin overly sensitive to the fleeting contact of his fingers. A crooked grin curved the corner of his mouth as he shifted his body down and sucked the lace into his mouth. His warm breath feathered across her hairless mound, sending flickers of erotic heat pulsing through her.

Oh ye gods! How much more of this could she stand? She lifted her hips up off the bed and wriggled the lace panties down over her hips.

Jackson chuckled softly and helped her to send the offending panties flying to the corner of the room before stroking one finger across the tiny bundle of nerves at the apex of her thighs.

Saralyn gasped for breath, closing her eyes tightly as desire spiralled through her. She bucked her hips upward while Jackson teased her mercilessly, circling one finger just inside the slick entrance to her sex and then withdrawing it again.

"More, damn it!" She didn't recall ever begging a man before.

"More what? More of this?" He eased a second finger inside her while moving the first back and forth across her clit.

Saralyn grabbed his wrist and forced his finger deep inside her. *Oh yeah. Much better.* "Don't be a bastard. You know what I want."

Jackson didn't bother to answer, but sat back on his heels to bury a second finger inside her. A darkly evil grin adorned his ruggedly handsome face.

Saralyn stared at his massive cock, hard and erect and promising to deliver everything she needed, everything she wanted. Part of her wanted to get up and run away, far from this man who could elicit such a pulse-pounding response from her without even trying. The other part of her wanted to impale herself on that delicious shaft. "Please." The word escaped her lips, soft and pleading.

"Now that's more like it." Jackson dipped his head to devour her lips. Was it possible for someone to be savage and gentle at the same time? His mouth moved over hers, plundering and worshipping in turn.

He shifted his weight, and Saralyn could feel the tip of his massive cock pressing against the damp entrance to her sex. It was the most intensely erotic sensation that she'd ever experienced. "Damn you!" She arched upward, trying to impale herself on his rigid shaft. "I need you inside me."

"And I need to be inside you." He cupped her face in his hands, staring straight into her eyes as he thrust deep, burying himself to the balls in her moist channel.

Reality blurred. All she could feel, all she could think about was the incredible sensations created by the movement of his cock inside her. He surged into her again and again. She could feel him, hot and huge, stretching her to the very limits. This was what she'd been missing all her life. Sex had never been so mind-blowingly intense, so exceptionally powerful. Every fiber of her being felt alive, every nerve quivered with erotic heat.

She moaned and whimpered as Jackson thrust into her again and again, groaning at each thrust as the tension between them escalated until the heat of their passion consumed her and a wave of pure sensual heat threw her up and over the edge into a fiery climax.

Jackson let out a shout of triumph, and thrust one last time, unleashing his own climax and filling her with his hot seed. They clung to each other for endless moments, unable to summon the energy to move. Finally, Jackson rolled over and lay beside her, one leg thrown carelessly across her thighs.

Saralyn felt good. Amazingly good. Replete. Satisfied. Totally and utterly spent. How had he managed to pull her so completely into his reality, so thoroughly into the sensual storm of his lovemaking? Never before had she lost herself so completely in the act of sex.

She sighed contentedly. Maybe later she'd worry about it. Right now, she just wanted to close her eyes and snuggle against Jackson's solid, reassuring bulk.

Chapter Three

"Hey, I found something!" Trace burst into the room and Jackson grabbed the sheet to pull it up over Saralyn's sleeping figure.

Normally it wouldn't matter that the guys were so casual about their personal space. "Ever heard of knocking?" It was hard to be mad in the face of Trace's boyish enthusiasm.

"Knocking? Why? Oh, sorry!" He had the grace to look ashamed for a total of thirty seconds. "But guess what I found in the enforcers' file server."

"My brother?" Saralyn poked her head out from behind Trace's shoulder. The hope in her voice was palatable.

"Um, not exactly. At least not yet. I found an internal memo and I think they're talking about you." He held out a tablet for Jackson to see. "If this is her, she really is what you thought."

"What you thought?" Saralyn frowned.

Trace had the tact of a two-year-old with an attention problem! Jackson glared at him, and then sighed as Saralyn waited for him to say something. "I think what Trace means is that I suspect you are one of the lost children. You knew that. It's doubtful that your abilities are the result of any kind of natural mutation, which leaves only gene splitting or a surgical implant to explain your exceptional talents." He turned to take the proffered tablet.

"Oh shit!" The face that stared at him from the screen was a slightly younger version of Saralyn. From the slight inconsistencies, he guessed it was a computer enhancement of an older picture, probably one from when she first escaped from the lab. There was no longer any doubt that she was indeed one of the lost children. A chain with a number hung around her neck. Seventy-two. That was her number, and most likely the only name the lab had gifted her with. The caption sent a chill right down to his toes.

Missing lab experiment. Reward for return, any condition. Dangerous. Do not attempt to apprehend. If seen call the nearest barracks and keep the subject in sight until help arrives.

He glanced at the date on the article. Just last month. Someone must have seen Saralyn and resurrected the search. Her picture would have been on the gallery of females at the arena where they'd rescued her. Maybe one of the enforcers had seen it and made the connection. He noted that they avoided referring to her as human, a tactic meant to dehumanize a target. It was easier to do bad things to people if you didn't consider them people. Not good. Not good at all.

"Can I see that, or are you trying to stare a hole through it?" The dry humor in Saralyn's voice brought a flicker of a smile to his face.

"I don't think you're going to like it. Never met a female yet that liked her own picture." He handed her the tablet.

Saralyn studied the picture in silence, hugging the blankets up around her shoulders. Trace shifted his weight from one foot to the other, not saying a word. He was a whole lot better with computers than people, especially people he barely knew like Saralyn.

"That doesn't leave a lot to discuss, does it?" She sighed, a heartbreaking sound. "If I'm one of those kids, I was an orphan that someone sold to them. I can't have a brother. I probably dreamed the whole thing up to make myself feel better."

"Maybe not. There's something else I found as well." Trace plucked the tablet out of her hands and tapped it a few times, pulling up a different picture. "This guy is about your age, and according to his file he was severely disciplined for leaving one of the lab doors unlocked. One of the lost children escaped, and while he managed to track her for a time across the lower parts of the town the subject eventually gave him the slip. That girl was never recovered and I'm betting that girl is you. The boy you remember may not be a blood relative, but he let you escape despite knowing he would be harshly reprimanded. Only his brilliance in the Provincial skirmishes a few years back managed to get his career back on track." He handed Saralyn the tablet. "This is the boy. Do you recognize him?"

Jackson watched the expressions chase each other across her expressive face as she stared at the tablet. Apprehension. Recognition. Jubilation. Uncertainty.

"Yes. That's him." She looked up. "He's not my brother, he was one of my keepers. I wonder if he ever wonders what happened to me. He never came back, but at least now I understand. If he did, he would have led the searchers right to me. It would have been like signing my death warrant. What's his name? I never even knew his name."

"Brice." Trace's face relaxed. "The enforcers don't use last names -- just their legion number. His is the forty-third division so he goes by Brice forty-three. He was promoted to head of the second squad just last month. That's about as high as you can get in the military without political connections."

"Do you think he'd want to see me again? Or does he regret having let me go." She chewed on her bottom lip, looking frail and uncertain.

Jackson slipped a comforting arm around her shoulder. "Who knows what an enforcer feels. How about we get some clothes back on?" He gave Trace a pointed look. "Maybe Trace can see what he can find out about this Brice and then we can discuss options. You don't want to go running right back into the hands of the guys who want you back in any condition. That's a fancy way of saying 'dead or alive'."

Saralyn nodded, pulling the sheet up to her chin.

"I'll get a full report on the guy and meet you in the strategy room, okay?" Trace took the tablet from her.

"Sounds good. How much time do you need?"

Trace shrugged, a confident grin on his face. "An hour, tops. Now that I have a name and a face it's like taking ammo from a squad of newbie guards."

"Well, make sure the guards don't know who's interested in them." The last thing Jackson wanted was to have a division of enforcers descend on their little hideaway. As it stood, the government troops had bigger fish to fry, so they conveniently ignored the ragtag groups of mercenaries plying their trade in the inner provinces.

Trace gave him a mock salute before ducking out the doorway, tablet in hand. "See you in the strategy room in one."

Jackson turned to Saralyn. "I suppose that means we'd better get up and get some clothes on. You want a shower before you get dressed?"

A slow, sensuous smile lit up her delicate features, and sent a blaze of heat curling through his groin. Her eyes danced with mischief as she put the tip of one finger in her mouth. "Sounds heavenly. Care to join me? We could save water and be good environmental citizens at the same time." She sucked on the finger suggestively.

"Hell yeah!" He threw the bedcover aside and scooped her up in his arms. "A good environmental citizen, that's me!" They were both deliciously naked, and he admired the soft caramel color of her skin against his own. Her soft skin glowed with a healthy sheen, contrasting sharply with the battle scars that crisscrossed his own tough hide. He had no idea why she hadn't slapped him silly the first time he'd dared to touch her, but since she appeared to find him desirable he didn't intend to give her enough time to rethink her decision.

Saralyn squealed, a happy sound that warmed Jackson's heart. "You are crazy! You know that, don't you?"

He managed to sear a passionate kiss across her lips, without shortening his stride. "Yes, ma'am. I do believe I am."

Reaching the bathing room, he used his elbow to slide the shower door open. He set her down on the floor and reached behind her to turn on the tap.

A cascade of warm water flowed from the large faucet built into the ceiling, and Saralyn tilted her head back to let the drops run down her face and shoulders, enclosing her body in a shimmery blanket of water.

Despite their recent lovemaking, Jackson's cock stirred at the sight of her glistening flesh, coming back to full attention as he stepped into the flow and pulled the little Asian beauty into his arms. Lowering his head, he licked the water from the tip of one pert breast.

"Mmmmm." Saralyn arched into his tongue, her breast pressing against his lips, and he obligingly opened his mouth to suck the succulent tip into his mouth.

She had perfect breasts, small but firm, with the tips tilting upward. He cupped them in his hands and divided his attention equally between the two. He licked and sucked in turn while Saralyn leaned into him, squirming and moaning beneath his hands. She tasted clean, with just a hint of some exotic herb that she must have rubbed on her skin. He couldn't quite place it, but it brought to mind visions of warm sensual places where men and women went to explore their passions.

Dropping to his knees, he worked his way down her delectable body. His tongue explored the dips and hollows of her hips, her belly, and came to rest on her mound. She quivered beneath his hands, responsive to his every touch. Parting the soft folds of skin guarding her sex, he inserted one finger into the warm depths of her sex.

Saralyn whimpered, pressing forward to force the finger deeper inside her. Jackson scored his thumb across her clit and she let out a low moan, her hips moving convulsively.

"That's it, baby. Give me all you got." Jackson crooned softly, holding her to him with an arm around her hips. Removing his finger, he fastened his mouth over her sweet mound. Sucking. Stabbing his tongue in and out. Grazing his teeth gently over her clit.

She exploded in his arms, letting out a high-pitched squeal of release as her climax ripped through her. The sound amplified, reverberating in the small enclosure.

Jackson surged to his feet, thrusting his stiff cock deep inside her pulsating sex. The muscles of her inner channel gripped him hard, and he shafted her with long deep strokes just as her climax began to subside. "Oh yeah. That feels so good." He wrapped his arms around her, holding her delectable body tight against him while the water cascaded over the both of them.

It didn't take long before his climax began to build, starting at the tips of his toes and washing up over him until his seed exploded from his cock to bathe the inside of her damp pussy.

Saralyn let out a strangled yelp as her second climax began, triggered by Jackson's own. She collapsed against him, and they both sunk slowly to the floor with the water pulsing all around them.

* * *

"So here's the thing." Trace looked uncomfortable.

Saralyn felt an anxious knot forming in her gut. Something wasn't right. Trace had been so excited and confident earlier, and now he seemed reluctant to give them any details. "Yes?"

"I found out some more about your Brice. I'm not so sure this is a guy you want to claim as a brother. The thing is, I was so stoked to find him, it didn't occur to me to wonder just how he managed to excel as an enforcer. Stands to reason it wasn't something good. The reason he got that promotion was because he managed to hunt down and execute a couple of people that were high on the government's wanted list." His voice dropped to barely above a whisper. "They pissed off the local governor by painting anti-government slogans on his garden wall, and he sent out a search and destroy order. Your... this guy... he found them, dragged them out into the middle of the street, and executed them. A shot through the back of the head for each. Brutal. The governor liked that part and promoted him on the spot."

Saralyn shook her head, the knot in her stomach solidifying into a cold hard lump. "No. It can't be." She looked at Jackson as if he could somehow make this nightmare stop. "It can't be true." She'd spent years trying to track this man down, and he was a cold-blooded murderer? He'd saved her. This didn't make sense.

Jackson draped a comforting arm around her shoulder. "Maybe we got the wrong guy. Or maybe he's changed since he saved you. It happens. Life can be harsh and some people just cave."

She bit her lip to prevent the tears she could feel forming behind her eyes. "I need to know. I have to find out what happened that day, and if he's my hero or my persecutor." She paused to gather her thoughts. "You all think I'm one of those kids? Well then, help me to find the truth. Help me to find out if I'm really that high on the government kill list. Please." Her voice cracked on that last word, sounding soft even to her own ears, and for some reason that pissed her off. She was tough. A survivor. She didn't cry over stupid things like lost dreams.

"So how do we do that?" Trace looked at Jackson. "I don't think walking up to the barracks and knocking on the door is a good idea."

"Probably not." Jackson's eyes narrowed in thought. "I think Saralyn needs to lay low until we figure this out. She could be in a whole lot of danger this close in to the enforcers' stronghold."

"I need to see this guy. If that puts me in a risky situation, so be it." Saralyn shrugged. "I have to do it."

"There is another way." Kaeden spoke up, and they all turned to look at him.

"What did you have in mind?" Jackson sounded hesitant.

Kaeden shrugged. "We go get this guy and bring him here."

Trace snorted. "That's our sarge. Always got a Plan B. Not always a good one, but a plan."

Kaeden put a hand up. "Not as crazy as it sounds. We hack the guy's schedule, find a point in the day where he's not surrounded by his enforcer pals, and pick him up. We can make sure he's under control, take him somewhere neutral and Saralyn can get some face time with him, see if he's the one she remembers. And, we can decide whether or not he ever gets to see her again."

"We're going to abduct an enforcer?" Jackson raised a sceptical eyebrow. "Do you think that's smart?"

"Smarter than waltzing into their stronghold and saying, 'Hi.' What do you think Saralyn's going to do if we don't? Just let the subject drop because it sounds a bit dangerous?"

"Good point." Jackson turned to Saralyn. "What do you think? You want to meet this guy?"

Well of course she did. Maybe. Somehow, she'd never pictured her brother as one of the bad guys. "I need to. The image of him leading those goons away from me is so clear, I need to know what happened that night. Maybe I have it all wrong and I should be running hard in the opposite direction, but I need to know. Am I one of the lost children, and if I am, then what?" She shook her head. "I have so many questions and I need the answers." She looked up at Jackson, hoping he'd understand. This wasn't something she could walk away from.

Jackson put his hand over hers, giving it an encouraging squeeze. "Then we'll get you some answers. Trace, can you get us this guy's schedule for the next few days?"

"Right here." Trace fiddled with the tablet, and then held it up so the group could see it. "His division is assigned to night patrol in the Northwest sector of the city for the next week."

"That's a rough section of town." Kaeden narrowed his eyes thoughtfully. "How do they work the patrols? Any chance of catching him on his own? We don't want to start a fight with the whole damn division or we'll be looking for a new home in one of the outlying provinces."

Trace shrugged. "We're going to have to get that info the old-fashioned way. Follow them and hope they split up at some point."

"We can go scout the area and find somewhere to take him once we pick him up. That end of the city is full of abandoned houses and shops." Snake spoke up for the first time. "I'll do that as soon as night falls, and let you guys know where to bring the target."

"We're all set then." Kaeden nodded at Saralyn. "We'll do our part, and when we find the guy, Jackson can bring you to the rendezvous point." He looked around the room. "We all good?" An assortment of grunts and yeahs sounded and he nodded. "Okay then. Meeting over."

Saralyn watched the mercenaries file out of the room. If she hadn't seen them working together to get Dee's little sister out of that compound, she wouldn't feel nearly as confident in their abilities to pull this off. They were a ragtag-looking bunch at best, but beneath those unassuming exteriors, she knew they had wills of iron and a multitude of useful skills.

Chapter Four

"You guys have no idea the trouble you are in."

Kaeden had to give the big guy credit for confidence. They'd used tranq guns to bring him down and the effects must still be in his system, but to listen to him you'd think he was on the verge of breaking his restraints and tearing all four of them to bits with his bare hands. As a precaution, they'd blindfolded him before stuffing him into the jeep and transporting him to the warehouse Snake had chosen. He looked over his shoulder. "You call Jackson?"

"Yup. Should be here any moment with the girl." Snake sauntered across the floor toward the captive. "Think we should pull the blindfold? Be interesting to see the look on his face when he sees her."

"Girl? This is about a girl?" Disbelief dripped from every word. "I have never done anything to a girl that she didn't ask for, and enjoy for that matter. You've got the wrong guy. If you let me go now, I'll let it drop. I understand wanting to protect a female."

"You don't understand jack, asshole." Pete let out a snort of laughter. "If we even thought you laid a hand on the girl, you wouldn't be sitting there in one piece."

"Then what the hell is the problem? This sure don't feel like any snatch and grab I've ever heard of."

"So how'd you manage to get a promotion? Rumor has it you offed a couple of kids who pissed off the governor. Not very nice." Barely restrained rage sounded in Pete's voice.

"They weren't kids, and they deserved what they got. Did the rumor happen to mention that the graffiti they drew was drawn in blood? Blood of a homeless guy who happened to be sleeping on a park bench in front of the wall? I didn't think so. It kind of takes away from the story, and the rags like a good story."

"Got any siblings?" Kaeden threw the question out, and they all watched the big guy for any kind of response.

"Siblings? Not that I know of. What kind of question is that?"

* * *

The sound of a door being opened echoed loud in the empty house, and the men all backed up a step. Saralyn appeared in the doorway with Jackson close behind her. She hesitated, her eyes fixed on the man in the chair, and she drew in a sharp breath. "That's him." She whispered the phrase in a hushed voice. "He's the one who saved me."

"Me? Saved you from what?" Exasperation sounded in Brice's voice. "Can someone tell me what the hell is going on here?"

"Why do you have him blindfolded?" Saralyn walked toward the chair, staring intently at Brice.

"Just a precaution." Jackson was right behind her, ready to move if anything or anyone threatened her. "If it turned out we had the wrong guy it would have been easiest to dump him if he didn't know who we were. No harm, no foul. Now though, I guess you two need to see each other." Reaching down, he undid the blindfold and pulled it off.

Brice blinked for a moment as his eyes adjusted to the light.

Saralyn stood quietly in front of him. Would he recognize her? How much had she changed from that little waif with the big brown eyes that he'd hidden in the dumpster? Had he even thought of her during all these long years?

"You!" The look of shock on his face was telling. He did remember her. "They told me you were captured and executed. All of you were. How on earth have you managed to avoid them all these years?"

"Avoid who? And what do you mean all of us? How many were there?" She felt Jackson's arms go around her and she leaned back gratefully against his comforting strength.

The man sighed heavily, shaking his massive head. "You don't remember the lab? Me? The other children? The experiments? Any of it?" Saralyn shook her head. "I will tell you, but you have to promise not to do anything dumb. It's over, and nothing you can do would make a difference now. If they get their hands on you, you're a goner."

"Difference to what?" Saralyn felt Jackson tense up behind her.

"To anyone. It's a long story. You might want to sit down."

Someone brought a chair forward, and Jackson sat down, pulling Saralyn into his lap. Some faint part of her smiled at the purely male gesture of possession. "So tell me. I've spent years trying to find you, but all I remember is that night. You shoving me into a dumpster and leading the troops away in the other direction."

Brice sighed. "Where to begin? What you remember is only the very end of the fiasco. There was this scientist who thought he could improve on people. He took his ideas to the government and they set him up in a lab. Now the only way to see if his ideas really worked was to experiment on people. So, they gathered up a bunch of homeless kids and took them to the lab. You were one of them. I was one of them. A lot of us didn't survive the experiments. In you, he implanted cybernetic enhancements that were supposed to make you a super-spy. Me, I got DNA from wild animals spliced into my genes to make me stronger, a better fighter. He had a lot of kinky ideas, a real mad scientist, if you get my drift. Thing is though, that once the enhancements started to work, we weren't eternally grateful to our tormentors. Some of us turned on them and others just refused to do what they were told. Add that to the fact that the costs were astronomical, it's no wonder the government decided to pull the plug."

"The lost children. They were real." Jackson tightened his grip on Saralyn as if he could take away her pain.

"Oh yeah. We are real." Brice shifted his weight. "Any chance you can loosen these restraints? I'm not going to do anything to you. Saralyn is like a sister to me, and you need to know the whole story if you're going to keep her safe." His voice hardened. "You are going to keep her safe, aren't you?"

"Oh yeah." Jackson looked up at her. "Even from you if I have to, so shut up and get on with the story. So far I'm not buying that you're the good guy in this."

Brice shrugged, relaxing a fraction. "When they decided to tank the project, they had to do something with the kids that were left. Boys like me, they put in the military where they could keep an eye on us. If we screwed up or turned out to be unstable they'd take care of us then. They had us under control. The girls though, were a different matter. They had various enhancements, and they were all young and had a tendency to think for themselves. When their hormones kicked in at puberty, their reactions to situations became wildly unpredictable. There was some concern that they might never be controllable so the government decided to terminate them all."

"They just decided to murder a bunch of helpless girls? Nice bunch of politicians we have." The grim look on Kaeden's face would have scared a lesser man.

"They tried." Brice corrected him. "A lot of those girls weren't as helpless as their jailers thought. Up to that point we kids had all been kept together in small groups. We were like family to each other. We came up with a mass escape plan, and it worked for a lot of us. Some of the kids were caught before they managed to get one foot outside the lab, but a lot of us managed to escape. That's the part you remember, Saralyn. We knew that if the boys were caught, they'd be disciplined but allowed to live, so we boys played along with the termination plan. We pretended we were okay with whatever they did to the girls so long as our necks weren't on the chopping block. The enforcers understood self-interest a whole lot more thoroughly than they understood family dynamics, so they bought it."

"Makes sense in a twisted kind of way." Jackson sounded dubious. "So, then what?"

"Every month, the troop divisions rotate. We figured that would be the perfect time to make a break. The troops most familiar with the area and us would be leaving and the incoming guys wouldn't have had time to familiarize themselves with the city or us. On day one of the next rotation, we waited until dusk and everyone made a break at the same time. The lab went into total chaos within minutes. We split into groups of two, one guy and one girl. If it looked like we were going to get caught, the female hid and the boy led the enforcers away from her under the pretext that he had been chasing her all along, trying to recapture her and she was just around the next corner." A crooked grin lit up his face. "It worked for a dozen of us. Those troops never understood that someone might give themselves up to protect another person. They didn't understand our allegiances, and we used that against them."

"So you did hide me and lead them off. That much is true, even if you aren't my brother." Saralyn stood and crossed the floor between them, shaking off Jackson's restraining hand.

"Yeah. I did. I just didn't realize it had done any good until now. Some of the other guys heard from the girls they'd helped, but you just disappeared. I assumed you'd been terminated."

Saralyn paused in front of him and turned to the group. "Can we untie him? He's not one of the bad guys."

Jackson frowned. "I'm not so sure. How do we know this isn't just a line of bull to save his ass?"

Brice frowned, looking thoughtful for a moment. When he spoke, though, he sounded surprised, as if the detail had just come back to him. "The dragonfly! We all have a dragonfly tattoo on our left ankle. The enforcers marked us with it when they brought us into the lab so they could be sure to tell us apart from normal children." Brice extended his leg. "Go ahead and look. I'll bet my life Saralyn has a matching one.

Saralyn looked over at Jackson, and he gave a slight nod of his head. He knew about the tattoo, he'd asked her about it the first time they'd made love. At the time, she'd answered honestly that she thought her parents must have had her tattooed before she'd been orphaned. The tattoo had been on her leg as long as she could remember. Turning back to Brice, she lifted his pant leg and peeled back the thick, military-issue sock.

There it was, an exact match for hers. A dragonfly tattoo.

Jackson let out a long breath. "Looks like he might be telling the truth, and my lady here seems to agree with him so I say we untie him and get a little more comfortable. Kaeden?"

The sergeant nodded. "Just so long as he remembers we still have a few tranquilizer darts left. Snake, you want to run over to that pub we passed a way back and get us some beer?"

"I'm on it! Pete, come ride shotgun for me." The two mercenaries jumped up and hustled out the door.

Saralyn took a step toward Brice, but Jackson stopped her. "I'll get this."

She knew he wasn't entirely convinced that Brice's concern for her was genuine, and she had to admit it felt good. Jackson cared about her for more than just a quick roll in the sack. She'd never let a man get close to her before, and she wasn't quite sure how Jackson had worked his way into her affections so completely in such a short period of time. Still, it felt good.

After Jackson loosened the bindings, Brice stood, rubbing the marks the restraints had left on his wrists. He made no move toward her, and Saralyn realized he knew Jackson would be upset if he did. It surprised her. Enforcers weren't known for their tact. Men! She wasn't sure if Jackson was protecting her, or just didn't want her that close to Brice now that he'd confirmed they weren't siblings. Still, it was nice to have someone care.

The door hinges squeaked loudly as Snake and Pete re-entered the room, carrying a couple of cases of beer they deposited on a dilapidated table.

Saralyn gave them a grateful glance before hooking her arm through Jackson's and approaching Brice. "You said some of the other guys had heard from the girls they helped escape. Are they still in touch?"

Brice looked pointedly around the room. "Do you trust these guys? Really trust them, I mean? Because if any of this gets back to the enforcers, people could die. People I care about."

Jackson spoke up, his voice a low snarl. "You're an enforcer, and we just let you loose. I think we're taking a bit of a risk here too."

Saralyn snorted in exasperation. "Yes I trust them with my life. You saved it back then, and they saved me more recently. So if the pair of you could quit staring each other down like a pair of dogs after the same bone, I'd appreciate it."

Jackson tensed for a second, then relaxed, letting out a bark of laughter. "Well said. Brice, you want a beer?" He took the case from Snake and Pete and started tossing cans to the group.

"Don't mind if I do." Brice popped the top and tipped the can back to guzzle the entire contents in one long slow gulp.

Jackson rolled his eyes, and opened his own can. "Okay. You can chug a beer better than me. I'll give you that one. So what about the other girls?"

Brice let out a loud belch. "There's half a dozen that I know of. The guys and I help them out from time to time. Because we're in the ranks of the enforcers, we can help them fly under the radar, give them advance warning when they're in danger. They're pretty skittish, though, even with us. The official government line is that they were all terminated long ago, but we all know that's a crock of shit. If the girls are ever caught it won't be pretty. If it comes right down to it, we'll do whatever it takes to protect them. Two of them are married to buddies of mine. They're easy to protect. No one looks for fugitives right under their noses. The ones we worry about are the ones like Saralyn there who are running around in plain sight. It's quite possible some might not even know what they are, just like her. One slip, one enforcer who sees the wrong thing at the wrong time, and they could get caught." He scowled at Saralyn. "I didn't even know you were alive. There could be scores of you out there that we aren't even aware of."

She nodded. It was true. She'd managed to block everything before the escape from her mind. There could be others, maybe a few or maybe a lot. There was no way to know for sure. "We need to look for them." Her brow furrowed. "We need to connect us all together so we can protect and hide each other. How do we start? I have no idea how to find them." She looked from Brice to Jackson. "Can you help?"

"It'll be hard." Brice spoke slowly, thoughtfully. "We need to be careful not to alert the authorities, but it can be done." He accepted another can of beer from Snake and popped the tab. "Are you sure you want to do this? It'd be easier for you to hide on your own. These guys would help you."

"These guys will help her no matter what she decides." Jackson sat down on an empty crate and drew her back down onto his lap. "She's family now, and we look after our own." He nuzzled her neck.

Brice nodded, looking satisfied with that answer. "Then I have to tell you that my pal Greg and I are already all over this. We track down leads, and if we find one of the girls we let her know that she isn't alone, that we are still here and still willing to help them whenever they need it. We have a meeting spot over on the outskirts of town where we meet once a month to share news and just generally hang out and catch up on each other's lives. The next meet is scheduled for next week. If you want, you and your guy can come meet the other girls. Sorry, but the rest of the team will have to stay behind. If a full-blown team of mercenaries descends on them, the girls will scatter faster than wheat in a windstorm."

"We'll think about it." Jackson gave Saralyn's shoulder a comforting squeeze. "I can see your point, but I'm not sure I'm comfortable going in without backup. I know I'm being paranoid, but it could be a trap."

Brice shrugged. "I know. It takes trust on both sides, and that's pretty hard to muster." A tiny bit of a smile curved the corner of his mouth. "Just an hour ago I was sitting here blindfolded so I can appreciate I'm not on your firm-fast-friend list quite yet. The offer is there though. And if you ever need to get a hold of me, just call and leave a message at the barracks. Tell them your name is Angel. That's the code name all the lost ones use when they need to contact me."

"Thanks. I appreciate that." Saralyn hopped off Jackson's lap and crossed to Brice, giving him a big hug and placing a chaste kiss on his cheek. "And thank you for saving my life."

"Oh hell." Jackson tossed his empty beer can into the far corner of the room, and sat up straighter. "We can go visit your sisters if you really want to. If Brice here wanted to betray us or hurt you he's had plenty of chance already. I'll just take lots of ammo with me."

Saralyn danced across the room to throw her arms around his neck. He really was an amazing guy. For the first time in her life she let herself wonder what the future might be like. A future with people she could trust, and a special guy that she could count on. A guy like Jackson.

* * *

"You're really sure this Brice is the same guy you remember?" Jackson brushed a stray strand of hair off her face. He shifted his position on the bed so that they lay facing each other.

"Yes. He's a lot older, but I'm positive. And some of the things he said about the lab and the experiments, they stirred up memories I'd forgotten about. They are really bad, so maybe I just didn't want to remember any of it except the part where he saved me." She traced her finger down his naked chest, stopping at his belly button.

After a short debrief session when they'd returned to the team's base house, she and Jackson had retired to his room. It had been a long day. As exciting as it was to finally meet the man she remembered as a brother and discover the missing parts of her past, the revelations had left her exhausted.

"I am going to sleep like a baby tonight." Saralyn yawned and snuggled up against him.

"Are you really tired?" Jackson slanted her a mischievous look.

Saralyn cocked an eyebrow at him. "Somewhat. Why? Did you have something in mind?"

He loved the way the sexy little witch played innocent when she couldn't possible mistake his meaning. His cock was painfully erect and pressing against her belly. "I thought we could both use a little bit of exercise to help us unwind before we go to sleep."

"Really." Saralyn feigned detached interest, and it was all he could do not to laugh out loud. Her eyes were full of a mischievous invitation. "You want to go jogging?"

"I was thinking of something a little less public." He lowered his head to nibble on the sensitive lobe of her ear. "Something like yoga, or swimming, or…" He used his tongue to trace a line down her jaw to the vulnerable hollow at the base of her throat.

Saralyn let out a gasp as his tongue hit just the right spot. "I might be willing to consider… a private event."

"Capital!" He rolled over on his back, pulling her up on top of him so that she straddled him. "Have you ever ridden a horse?" He loved the way her eyes widened as his intentions sank in. She truly was a witch. A sexy, self-assured, dark-eyed witch who could turn his world upside down with a single glance.

"There are not a lot of horses in the city. I'm afraid that's one skill I've never mastered." She circled his shaft with her fingers and gave it a long, slow pull. "But I've always wanted to learn."

Rising on her knees, she positioned his cock at the entrance to her sex and lowered herself slowly, inch by agonizingly erotic inch over the massive shaft. "Oh, that is so…" The sentence trailed off unfinished as she used one finger to trace the contours of his belly with a deliberate possessiveness that sent heat exploding through every nerve in his body.

He bucked his hips slowly, encouraging her to ride him in a deliciously sexy manner that left him groaning softly. Passion flared in her lovely eyes and she leaned forward to clutch at his shoulders as she began to move up and down in time with his thrusts.

"Oh God, Jackson. Jackson!"

"I know, baby. I know what you need, what we both need." He muttered the words softly, his voice raw with hunger.

He could feel the walls of her channel begin to quiver at the beginning of her climax, and he grasped her hips, ramming himself deep up inside her again and again. A fierce need urged him on, faster and faster until the tumultuous climax overtook them both, leaving them shaken and gasping for breath.

Saralyn collapsed on top of him, and he wrapped his arms around her, not sure if he was holding on to her for his sake or hers.

Tomorrow they would start the dark journey to reclaim her past, but for now they had each other. They were together. It was enough.

Riding Shotgun (Mercenaries 3)

Anne Kane

Kalie's a genetic experiment who was never supposed to get out of the lab. If the government finds her, they will kill her without hesitation. She's a crack shot, though, and she's used to looking out for herself.

Kalie's affinity for all things mechanical helps her make a living on the underground street racing circuit, but it's a dangerous game, and lately things haven't been going so well.

Shotgun falls hard from the first time he meets Kalie, and he's determined to make her his own. When accidents keep plaguing her car, he gets suspicious. With the help of his mercenary buddies he's determined to find the source of the problem and keep his woman safe.

Chapter One

A subtle movement on the far ridge caught Shotgun's attention. It could be a deer on the far ridge, but he doubted it. Moving the scope of his rifle in a slow sweep, he searched for the cause. There. On the west slope. A faint flash as the late afternoon sun reflected off a metal surface.

He kept the rifle trained on the spot, his trigger finger itching, and sure enough, there she was. A sharpshooter. Her rifle looked suspiciously similar to his own, and she handled it like a pro. Her mistake had been not making sure all the shiny metal was covered up.

Her outfit blended well with the surrounding rocks and he had to give her credit for finding a good vantage point. She'd managed to position herself in a wide crack in between two large outcrops of rock. Her back was protected by a sheer wall of granite. An irregular jumble of boulders in front of her gave her numerous places to rest the barrel of her rifle.

He recognized her from the portfolio Brice had shown them of the *Lost Children*. Kalie. Her riotous mop of long dark curls was held back behind a wide hairband, and the camo outfit she wore covered her deliciously ripe curves. He was too far away to see if her eyes really were as dark and sensual as they looked in her picture, but he was sure it was Kalie.

Her undivided attention was on the gathering in the clearing below. That would be her second mistake. Just because you're hunting, doesn't mean you aren't also being hunted. As he glanced around, gauging the distance between them and the amount of cover available, he felt the corner of his mouth lift in a slow grin.

Nothing like a bit of a challenge to liven up the evening.

* * *

The man came out of nowhere. Jerking her rifle out of her hands, he flipped her over and slammed her body into the ground. The breath whooshed out of her in one long exhale as he pinned her to the ground with his superior weight. Instinctively, she tried to bring her knee up to fend him off.

"I don't think that's such a good idea, little girl." His voice was low, a thread of humor running through it as he blocked the move with a casual flick of his leg. He could afford to be amused. He was planted firmly on top of her, and her rifle was no longer snugged comfortingly against her chin. She eyed up the distance to the weapon. Too far.

A fierce anger enveloped her, fueled by an unfamiliar feeling of helplessness. No one snuck up on her like that. No one. Taking a deep breath, she forced her body to relax. She could get out of this. If he thought she'd given up, he'd let his guard down.

"Who are you?" She spat the words out between clenched teeth, betraying her fury. So much for letting him think she'd given up.

"Name's Shotgun, Kalie. I'm with Saralyn down there, and her new beau. Just kind of keeping an eye on the situation when I noticed you over here. I don't like people watching my friends through the scope of a rifle."

"Really?" He knew her name. Shit. He probably knew about the other girls as well. Her sisters. That couldn't be good. She needed to neutralize him quickly and let them know they'd been found out. She shifted her weight, as if trying to get more comfortable. "Well,

I don't like people skulking around watching my friends either, so I guess we're even. Would you mind getting off me? You're heavy."

"Not quite yet." He somehow managed to transfer both of her wrists to one hand. Raising his other arm, he spoke into the comm unit strapped around his wrist. "I got some action up here, Sarge. Little girl, with a big gun. Name of Kalie. Says she's watching point for the others. You want to verify that?"

"Should have expected something like this." Sarge's voice crackled over the unit. "I'll have Jackson check with the girls. Bring her on down, and we'll see if her story checks out."

"Roger that. Be down in a few."

Shotgun looked down at her. He was a big man. Big and hard. His face was all hard angles and planes, with a faint scar running down one side of his temple. She could feel hard muscles pressing into every inch of her. There wasn't a single soft spot on his entire body. Was he enhanced? One of the soldiers they'd fed those experimental drugs to during the provincial wars? That would explain how he'd managed to sneak up on her without her hearing him.

As she watched, a mischievous light danced in the depths of his eyes. He certainly didn't seem to think she was much of a threat. Maybe she could use that to her advantage

"Looks like we're going to join the party. Up you get." He surged to his feet with an innate grace that told her he'd kept up his training after the wars. Holding out a hand to help her up, he still managed to keep that rifle pointed directly at her.

"Fine. Let's get moving." She ignored the outstretched hand and stood. "Can I have my rifle back now, please?"

"Has sentimental value, does it?"

"Yeah." She smiled sweetly. "I've killed three assholes with it so far, and it's itching to loose a bullet on the fourth."

Shotgun snorted. "I think I'll hang on to it for now." Scooping the weapon up, he slung it across his back and gestured for her to move out.

She would have been shocked and just a little bit disappointed if he'd actually given her the rifle. No decent soldier would be that naïve. She eyed up the path she'd used to climb up here, but an imp of mischief made her reject it. Let's see how good that training was. Ignoring him and his rifle, she proceeded to follow the most difficult route to the valley floor.

It took them twenty minutes of fancy footwork and a couple of controlled skids before they reached the bottom. She had to grudgingly admire the way he managed to keep up while carrying both of the rifles, one of them trained on her. The next time she managed to land herself in a fight she wouldn't mind having him at her back.

Shotgun was right behind her as she marched into the middle of the clearing. Heads swiveled and she saw more than one jaw drop in shock. She hadn't been in close contact with any of her sisters since that last day in the labs, and they'd probably consigned her to the list of unfortunates who hadn't made it out. She'd told herself it was better that way.

Much as she wanted to forget, the memory of those labs was engraved on her mind. The scientist running them was truly mad. He convinced the government he could create super soldiers out of ordinary people. So, they gathered up a bunch of disposable kids for him to experiment on. She was one of the unfortunate children, as were most of the people in this clearing. In her case, the weird and extremely painful experiments had given her an affinity for anything mechanical. There wasn't a car, a bike, or any other mode of transportation that didn't respond positively to her touch.

He'd expected her to be grateful. He'd expected them all to be grateful to him for the pain and suffering he inflicted on them. He'd watch them sometimes, while his assistants tortured them, his face as expressionless as if he were looking at a bug under a microscope. She still got cold shivers when she thought about his face.

Some of the kids turned on their tormentors and others just refused to do what they were told. Add that to the fact that the costs were astronomical, it was no wonder the government decided to pull the plug on the program. The boys were put in the military where the government could keep an eye on them.

The girls though, were a different matter. They had an unfortunate tendency to think for themselves, and when their hormones kicked in at puberty, their reaction to situations became wildly unpredictable. There was some concern that they might never be controllable so the government decided it would be best to terminate them all.

Luckily for her and the other girls, that plan had gone extremely poorly for the powers that be. No one knew how many of the girls had escaped.

"Kalie?" It was more of a question than a statement. The woman staring at her in shock had changed a lot since those days in the lab, but Kalie still recognized her.

She took a deep breath. "Yeah, Winter. It's me."

"Kalie!" This time her name was a squeal of delight as her former bunkmate enveloped her in a bear hug. "We thought you were dead!"

"Easy! You're going to kill me yourself if you keep squeezing that hard." She couldn't keep the joy out of her voice. She'd missed them so much.

"So who's your friend with the guns?" Winter took a step back, eyeing up Shotgun.

"Not my friend." She turned to glare at Shotgun. The fact that he just smiled cheerfully did not improve her mood. "Ask Saralyn and her new beau. Apparently he's with them."

"He needs to learn not to point weapons at things he doesn't intend to shoot at." Winter frowned disapprovingly.

"She's one of us, Shotgun. You can put the gun down." Saralyn came rushing over to hug the new arrival. "It's been forever, Kalie. Where were you hiding all this time?"

Kalie hugged her back, savouring the unexpected joy of being one of the group again. She'd been on her own for so long, she'd forgotten how good it felt. "In the racing pits, where else? With my ability to coax the best out of my ride, I make enough to keep me in beer, but not enough to attract attention."

No one asked her why she hadn't contacted them before now. They just accepted her. They weren't blood siblings but she considered them all to be her sisters. Sisters of the heart.

Out of the corner of her eye, she saw Shotgun click the safety back on and lower his rifle before he moved off to talk to the tall dark-haired guy who'd been with Saralyn. After marching her into the clearing at gunpoint, he thought he could just walk away without even apologizing? Now why did that annoy her? She turned her attention back to Winter and Saralyn. "So what have you girls been up to?"

By the time Kalie had greeted each of the girls, Shotgun had disappeared.

Damn.

* * *

"Sounds like a great idea." Shotgun answered Jackson automatically, his attention on the girl he'd tackled up on the cliff. Kalie sauntered across the clearing, arm in arm with one of the other girls. Her tight-fitting outfit outlined her luscious curves with groin-tightening detail. She'd twisted her hair up in a ponytail, a streak of brilliant blue weaving through the long dark tresses.

His gaze fell to her shapely ass, and his cock twitched as he remembered how she'd felt beneath him. An image flashed through his mind, of her lying across the rocks up on the cliff, holding the rifle, caressing it almost. Now that he'd confirmed she wasn't the enemy, he had to admit she stirred something deep inside him that he hadn't known existed anymore. Something fierce and protective. Something lustful.

"So you'll back me up when I talk to Sarge?" Jackson slapped him on the back. "Thanks!"

"Sure. No problem." He sure hoped he hadn't agreed to anything outrageous. With Jackson, you never knew what you were getting into. He remembered the time the wily mercenary had convinced them all to go to a party in the next province. Hopefully whatever he'd just agreed to wasn't that dangerous. "Excuse me."

He quickened his pace, angling to intercept Kalie and Winter. Was it his imagination, or did she slow her pace to allow him to catch up?

"Hey there. How's it going?"

Kalie slanted an inscrutable look from under her lashes. "Going just fine. Where did you disappear to in such a hurry back there?"

So she'd been looking for him. "Just had to check in with Jackson, make sure I was clear for the rest of the day."

"And?"

"And what?"

"Are you free for the rest of the day?"

"Oh, yeah. The group's on stand-down for now."

"What group is that?"

He realized she had no idea who he was, or what he did. Did he want her to know? He couldn't recall the last time he'd even cared about someone's opinion of him or his life choices. "I work with a group of ex-soldiers. We fought together during the Provincial wars, and kind of stuck with each other when they were over." He shrugged. "We're good at soldiering and it pays the bills."

"Winter says you only take jobs you believe in."

So she'd been asking questions about him. "Yeah." He fell into step beside her. "I'm the company sharpshooter, and Jackson over there is the tech expert. There are six of us in all."

"Must be nice to do something you believe in."

He detected a trace of wistfulness in her voice. "Yes, it is. So you race cars?"

"Yeah. Usually I do pretty well, although there's been a few bizarre accidents lately." Her brow furrowed for a moment, then she seemed to shake off whatever was bothering her.

"Maybe I could come watch you sometime?" He tried to keep his voice casual, but the thought of this woman controlling a couple thousand pounds of pulsating engine and metal was enough to make his mouth water and his cock stiffen. What else could she control?

She shook her head. "Street races aren't advertised. Even I don't know the locations until race day."

"Too bad. I'd love to see you in action." He made a mental note to have Trace check and see what he could find out about the street-racing scene. Nothing was buried deep enough to keep Trace out.

She turned and stared straight into his eyes. One shapely brow lifted and the beginnings of a smile crooked the corner of her mouth. "I bet you would. Love to see me in action, that is."

The challenge in her voice was unmistakable, as was the gleam in her eyes. She had the biggest, softest, darkest eyes he'd ever seen and right now they were glowing with desire. Shotgun didn't wait for her to rescind the invitation. Wrapping an arm around her waist, he pulled her to him and lowered his head to claim her mouth.

Chapter Two

Heat flooded through Kalie's body as Shotgun thrust his tongue into her mouth. She had the feeling that everything about this man was aggressive, but that was okay. She didn't do gentle. Nothing in her life led her to expect anything except what she fought for and took for herself. Right now she wanted Shotgun. Wanted him so bad she was tempted to take him right here, in front of all her sisters. Insanity.

His mouth moved over hers, tasting, exploring. Claiming. His tongue delved into every crevasse, every space. His arms tightened around her, as if he thought she might actually try to escape.

She kissed him back with a deep hunger that raged out of control. She wasn't like this. Never did this. Her life was all about control, about making sure that no one was in a position to hurt her ever again. What was it about this man that broke through all those self-imposed barriers?

"My truck is parked down the road." The skin of her neck muffled his words as he nibbled his way up toward her ear. "We need some privacy."

She could have ended it there. Should have ended it there. This was too much, too intense. Her legs felt like they'd buckle if he let her go. "Let's go."

She wasn't sure how they managed to get away from the group, how she managed to propel herself all the way down the narrow gravel road and around the corner. As soon as they were out of sight, Shotgun scooped her up in his arms and reclaimed her mouth.

Damn. Where had her sense of propriety gone? It would be obvious to everyone why they'd disappeared. Then again, who cared? What she wanted right now was to feel that long stiff shaft of his buried deep inside her. It had been too long since she'd let herself relax enough to enjoy a rousing good time with a man.

Shotgun managed to put her down on her feet without giving up possession of her mouth. He yanked down the tailgate of the truck and reached in to drag a blanket across the bare metal. Hopping up onto the blanket, he pulled her down onto his lap.

Damn. This was insane. She hadn't had sex on the tailgate of a truck since, well, never. Just the thought was a turn-on, as if they were a couple of teenagers too horny to find a better place.

As if he could read her mind, Shotgun relinquished her lips, his voice harsh with repressed desire. "We could go find a motel or something?"

Kalie shook her head. Hell, she grew up in a laboratory. Why bother to get prissy now, especially since her hormones seemed to be in overdrive around this guy? She needed to get him out of her system. Reaching down, she grabbed the bottom of her shirt and pulled it over her head.

Shotgun let out a low whistle. "Don't play around, do you, little girl?" Raising his hands, he cupped her naked breasts, kneading them softly before sucking one tightly pebbled tip into his mouth.

"I'm not a little girl." Kalie stated the obvious, closing her eyes as she savored the feeling of Shotgun's mouth on her skin. Her gut did a long slow glide down into the depths of desire. She leaned into him, instinctively seeking the shelter of his strong arms. He was so large, so solid. Just for once it was nice to let her guard down and not worry about getting caught.

He took his time, worshipping her breasts with his lips and tongue, swirling a path around the sensitive tips. He grazed his teeth across the nipple, then licked the pain away. Running one hand possessively down her back, he held her prisoner to his demanding mouth.

She could feel the thick length of his cock through the material of her jeans, and an imp of mischief made her wriggle her bottom. Shotgun rewarded her by sliding his hand down to give her a sharp slap on the ass. She let out a yelp of protest, more on principal than because it actually hurt. Truth be told, it felt kind of good.

"Damn, you taste good, little girl." He caressed her ass through the denim for a moment before bringing his hand around the front to fumble with the fastenings at her waist. Impatient to feel his naked skin against her, Kalie brushed his hand away and undid it herself. Sliding off his lap, she quickly shimmied her legs free and tossed the jeans into the back of the truck.

Shotgun stood and managed to divest himself of his remaining clothes in record time before pulling her back to him. "You're right. You're not a little girl, now are you?" Scooping her into his arms with restrained eagerness, he laid her down on the blanket and followed her into the bed of the truck. Propping himself up on one elbow, he used his mouth and hands to explore her body with a fierce thoroughness that took her breath away. He looked so rough and yet his hands were infinitely tender as he parted her thighs and lowered his head to nibble at the soft skin of her inner thighs.

His warm breath feathered across the soft folds of skin guarding her sex, and she let out a little whimper. Wrapping her fingers in his hair, she arched her back, mutely offering herself to him. She wanted him. Needed him. Wanted to feel the thick length of him plundering her moist channel. Needed to feel him inside her.

"Damn you to hell. Fuck me. Now." She gasped the words out as darts of liquid pleasure raced across the surface of her skin.

He raised his head, his dark eyes fixing on hers as a slow, knowing smile curved the corners of his lips. He didn't acknowledge her outburst, didn't reply. Bringing his hand to his mouth, he kept his gaze locked on her as he slowly licked one long finger and then inserted it deep inside her.

Kalie let out a strangled whimper as his thumb brushed across the tiny bundle of nerves at the apex of her thighs while his finger sent curls of lust dancing through every nerve ending.

He inserted a second finger and began to pump them in and out, his gaze never leaving her face. "Come on, little Kalie. Show me how hot you are. I want to feel you come apart in my hand."

Kalie closed her eyes and gave herself up to the desire swirling through her. It had been so long, so very, very long since she'd allowed herself to abandon all caution and enjoy the needs of her body. Her inner muscles started to spasm, grasping at the fingers and trying to draw them deeper inside. A wave of intense pleasure rolled through her, building itself into the perfect storm that raised her up to the stars and threw her over the edge. She let out an inarticulate scream, her hands opening and closing convulsively as pleasure rolled through her in consecutive waves.

When she was able to take a breath, she opened her eyes to find Shotgun staring down at her, his dark eyes glittering with desire. A wickedly lustful smile lit his eyes, and he circled his cock with one hand, slowly stroking the length.

"So. You're not a little girl after all." The smile widened, and Kalie felt the moisture begin to gather inside her in reaction to the lust she saw there. "Have you ever wondered what it would be like to ride Shotgun? I promise you'll enjoy the ride."

Kalie blinked as his meaning sunk into her lust-befuddled brain. He rolled over on his back, his muscular legs splayed wide as he slowly stroked his hand down the length of his massive cock.

Oh yeah. She wanted to ride Shotgun.

Rolling over, she got to her knees and straddled the big mercenary's hips. A glistening bead of pre-cum decorated the head of his cock. She reached out with one finger and touched the tempting droplet, bringing it to her lips.

Shotgun's eyes were glued to her face as she slowly licked the single drop from her finger. The feeling of power that washed over her as he let out a long groan was heady. He might be bigger and stronger and faster than her, but right now she held his very being in her power.

Rising to her knees, she guided the tip of his cock to the wet entrance of her sex. With infinite slowness she sank down, impaling herself on the thick shaft. She savored every inch as he invaded her channel, stretching her impossibly wider and scraping along nerves that hadn't quite recovered from the assault of his fingers.

She gave herself over to the moment, throwing her head back as his cock penetrated her body. He speared her with agonizing slowness, deeper and deeper, in a long slow slide until her buttocks rested against his balls. The heat from his body rose, inciting a desire deep within her, and she began to ride him. She set the rhythm slow at first, but soon the desire was more than she could handle. She began to move faster, sliding up and down, his cock slipping in and out of her slick sex. The friction caused a million tiny nerve endings to ignite in flames that roared through her entire body.

She whimpered and circled her hips, wanting to feel every inch of him, to make sure she didn't miss anything as the familiar heat began to surge up within her. She gave herself up to him then, his hips thrusting up into her, his heat rising to envelope her in flames as another orgasm began to build, taking away everything but the feeling between them.

Shotgun grasped her hips, holding her still as he plunged up into her, his face contorted in pleasure. "Hang on, darling, I'm coming." He thrust upward one last time, and she felt his cock jerk as his hot seed spilled into her.

The heat of his release triggered her own orgasm, and she gasped for breath as it rocked through her with the force of a volcanic eruption, sending waves of hot pleasure roaring through her. She collapsed on top of him, his cock still buried deep inside her.

He caged her in his arms, holding her tight as tiny aftershocks rippled through them both. She felt safe lying there, totally naked in his arms, and if she thought about it the fact might scare her. So, she decided not to think about it. For one glorious segment of time, she was just going to lie here with her head on the shoulder of the sexiest male she'd ever set eyes on.

Later, she'd let reality drift back in. Later.

* * *

Kalie gripped the steering wheel tightly in both hands and let her senses flare out. There it was again, that tiny quiver in the engine's rhythm that signalled a problem. The pressure in the cylinders wasn't holding steady. Every so often, it wavered just enough to interfere with the car's performance.

Damn! It felt like the head gasket was dissolving but that just wasn't possible. She'd replaced it less than a month ago, and even under race conditions it should be good for years. What the hell?

These glitches had been occurring with greater frequency lately, and it worried her. She "felt" the weakened area, mentally crossing her fingers. It had been fine before the race started, so with a bit of luck and some careful driving she should be able to finish the race without incident. That meant not going full out in the last few minutes to leave her competition in the dust.

She glanced in her rearview mirror. The kid in the black car had been pushing her hard for the past few miles. She'd intended to use the last straight to leave him choking in her dust, but the weakened gasket made that a bad plan. If she revved the engine too high, it might just blow.

If she kept to the inside on the next corner, she should be able to stay in the lead without risking the engine. She took a deep breath, and concentrated on the road.

The kid took the corner wide, losing ground but he was good. He got the car under control, and she could see him looming in her mirror. The finish line came in sight, and she calculated her odds. She didn't need a spectacular win. She just needed to come in ahead of the black car.

The vibration in the engine escalated. Shit. She eased back on the throttle a hair, keeping one eye on her competitor. The buildings on both sides of the improvised track flashed by in a blur. She could make it. She knew she could. She gritted her teeth. One mile to go.

It seemed like an eternity. She could see the black car inching up on her left side. She roared over the finish line with less than a half-car lead. Way too tight for comfort.

Easing up on the throttle, she feathered her brakes and made a wide loop to bring the car into the parking lot. When it finally shuddered to a halt, she let out the breath she'd been holding and slumped against the steering wheel. That had been way too close for comfort. She'd been the odds-on favorite in this race, and it should have been a walk in the park. She didn't like close finishes, and she didn't like surprises when it came to her car.

"You cheating bitch, get out of that car."

Kalie jumped as the driver from the black car banged both fists down on her side window, his face contorted with rage. What the hell was going on? First the car started having problems when it shouldn't, and now this? The last thing she wanted to deal with right now was a kid throwing a temper tantrum because he'd lost.

It got weirder. Shotgun materialized behind the kid, grasping his arms behind him. "I think you need to calm down, feller."

Shotgun? What was he doing here? And how had he known where to find her? She sure as hell hadn't told him about the race. After their little tryst, she hadn't expected to see him again. Did life ever get any easier? She released the door hatch and clambered out of her car, eyeing the kid with contempt. Sore losers didn't get far in this business. "You lost. Get over it."

Shotgun looked every bit as good as she remembered, and for some reason that pissed her off. She'd convinced herself that last night's little dalliance had been a combination of hormones and poor judgment. Apparently not, or else her hormones and judgment issues weren't ready to say goodbye to him yet.

"I was supposed to win. They told me it was a set deal," the kid snarled at her, while twisting helplessly in Shotgun's grasp.

"A set deal?" She stopped, turning her full attention on him. "They said I was going to throw the race? I never throw a race. Who told you that?"

The kid stilled, his eyes going wide. Seemed he'd just realized he'd made a tactical error. "No one. It was no one. It's just you're a girl. Who can't beat a girl?" His voice rose to an ear-shattering wail. "They're never going to let me on the circuit again."

Kalie looked at Shotgun and gave a slight shake of her head. "Let him go. If he's stupid enough to think he was going to win just because he's got a dick, he's not worth talking to. And if he believed I'd throw the race, he's even stupider."

Shotgun smiled, and there was absolutely no warmth in it. "The lady said to let you go so I will. I understand that she needs to be respected. If I ever, ever see you anywhere near her again, it's going to take more doctors than you can find in this city to put you back together again. Are we clear on that?"

"Yeah." The kid nodded vigorously, keeping his eyes focused on the pavement. "I didn't mean nothing by it. Just upset because I lost, you know?"

"No. I don't. Now get your sorry ass out of my sight." Shotgun shoved the kid aside hard, not paying any attention as the hapless driver landed on his hands and knees. He scrambled to his feet and took off into the shadows at the corner of the lot.

Shotgun's smile was decidedly warmer as he reached out to tuck a stray lock of hair behind Kalie's ear. "Nice driving. Want to go out for a celebratory drink?"

She looked down at her car. "Sounds like a hell of an idea. Just let me go collect my winnings."

He reached out and pulled her toward him, lowering his head to ghost an achingly sweet kiss across her lips. "I'll wait right here."

That was a kiss? She pulled his head down and fastened her lips on his, devouring his mouth with all of the frustration that had been building since these incidents with the car had begun three months ago. When she let him go, the dazed look on his face gave her a fleeting moment of satisfaction. Maybe he'd stop referring to her as a little girl now!

Chapter Three

Shotgun lounged against the wall of the garage as Kalie slid out from beneath her car and stood up, a wrench dangling loosely from one hand. She probably had no idea how adorable she looked with a smear of grease across one cheek. She looked surprised to see him.

"Did you want something?" The distantly polite note in her voice was a far cry from the passionate screams he'd managed to elicit from her the other night. This girl played major hard to get. She'd jump into his arms willingly enough when she wanted some action, but getting her to open up about herself, to let him inside her head, now that was a whole different matter.

"Just thought I'd hang around a bit, watch you work on the car." If you'd asked him last week if he believed in love at first sight, he would have laughed. Maybe that romantic bullshit was okay for Sarge or Jackson. Sure. They'd both fallen fast and hard for their gals. But he was different. Hardnosed. Pragmatic.

He'd seen too much, done too much. He wasn't the kind of guy a woman would want to keep in her life. He knew that and he was okay with it. The women he occasionally took to bed knew the score. He was just scratching an itch. Nothing permanent about it.

Then came Kalie. The first time he'd touched her, holding her down on the ground while he disarmed her, he'd felt a curious shifting in his chest. She was different. Together, they were different. He'd known she was telling the truth long before he marched her down that cliff, because he couldn't possibly feel this way about a woman who wasn't one of the good ones.

Yeah, he was falling in love with her. And that was okay. She needed him. Needed him to look after her. Even if she didn't realize it yet.

She cocked her head, a frown marring the perfection of her forehead. "Why?"

He smiled, letting her see the gentler side of him. Hiding the side that wanted to rip her clothes off and bury himself deep inside her again and again, until he was finally sated. Only he'd never be sated, never have enough of her. "Because a woman with a wrench just turns me on, little girl."

She arched an eyebrow. "I thought we established that I'm not a little girl."

He grinned. She wasn't about to let him get away with anything. "Oh yeah. We did that, but maybe I need a reminder?"

She stared at him for one long moment, and he held his breath. Then she laughed, the sound musical in the grimy garage. "Nice try but I have work to do. The left cylinder head gasket is going on this pile of crap, and replacing it is not fun. Especially considering I already replaced it less than a month ago."

It was his turn to frown. "I'm no grease monkey, but aren't those things supposed to last longer than that? Like years longer?"

She nodded grimly, the humor gone as quickly as it had arrived. "Yeah. They are. Something strange is going on here, and I don't like it. This isn't the first perfectly good part to fail at a critical time."

"A critical time? What do you mean?"

She sighed. "It started to give way during the race yesterday. That's why I laid off at the end and let that kid get so close to me. If I'd opened the car up full in the home stretch, the engine would have blown sky high."

They said it was a done deal. The kid's words echoed in Shotgun's mind. Suddenly the identity of the people who'd told the kid that took on a whole new importance. "Who has access to your car? Who would have been able to sabotage it?"

Kalie shook her head. "No one. I work on it myself, and the only person who gets remotely near it is the guy who fuels me up before the race. He's just a kid, and I'm not sure he could identify the parts of the engine, let alone sabotage them."

"What else has been going wrong lately? You mentioned this was just the last in a series of incidents."

She shrugged. "Other parts' failures. Tires shredding their steel belts. Bits of metal snapping when they shouldn't. Anyone else would just call it a run of bad luck…" She squirmed uncomfortably.

"But?"

"But I know better. When I put my hands on the car, I can feel it working. I would know if there's a problem. Like Saralyn can read the computers by touch, I have an affinity for machines. I should be able to tell if there is a problem and my car should never, ever have issues during a race. Ask anyone. My rep is built on what they think is my amazing luck with the cars."

He stared at her shrewdly. "Does anyone else know about your abilities?"

She shook her head. "No one who wasn't in that lab with me. I'm not dumb enough to risk my life by bragging. Which means I can't go accusing anyone of anything without explaining why I think something is going on." She sighed "And then there's the fact that no one should be able to get near my car. Maybe I'm just going crazy." She looked up. "I have no idea why I'm telling you all this."

He grinned again. "Because I'm your very own Prince Charming and I'm going to solve all of your problems?"

She smiled ruefully. "Yeah. And then we'll live happily ever after in a great big palace full of antique muscle cars."

He nodded slowly. "Okay. I was thinking we could live in a little house in the woods with a white picket fence and a station wagon full of kids, but if you want a palace..."

She wrinkled her nose. "A station wagon full of kids? Seriously?"

He flashed her his sexiest smile. "Well, since we seem to have trouble keeping our hands off each other, there's going to be a passel of kids involved, which means we'll be needing a station wagon. Or maybe a minivan."

Kalie rolled her eyes. "Suddenly the gasket seems like the least of my worries. Why didn't you tell me you were delusional?"

Shotgun shrugged and paced across the distance between them. "I find girls tend to stick around longer if they think I'm at least reasonably sane. But, to get back to the car problems, is there anyone with the opportunity to sabotage your car? Or a motive, for that matter?"

"Well, the motive is easy. Anyone who wants to beat me in a race." She paused, chewing thoughtfully on her bottom lip. "Or wants to make sure I don't qualify for the season's big windup race next month."

"Tell me about that one. How do you qualify?"

"The bookie decides based on your performance in the races throughout the summer. If you win enough, and the bettors like your style, then you get an invite. A maximum of twenty drivers compete, because the roads they run are on the outer circles and any more would be too dangerous. The route is different each year, so the drivers can't prepare in advance. It's a hundred miles of the toughest racing in the Provinces." She paused. "I've run it three years in a row now, and until recently I thought I might have a chance to win it this year."

"What's the payoff?"

She shrugged. "Enough cash that I'd never have to worry again. My rep would be made solid."

Shotgun let out a soft whistle. Money was a huge motivator, even without the prestige of winning something this big. "Sounds serious. I know a lot of lowlifes who would create major mayhem for a lot less."

She nodded. "Yeah, but how? No one but me goes near my car."

"Let me think on it. There must be something here you're overlooking. In the meantime, what kind of plans do you have for tonight?"

She blinked. "Tonight? None. Why?"

"Because I'd like to introduce you to my teammates. Saralyn is planning a barbeque to celebrate Jackson's birthday and I told her I was bringing you with me."

She arched one of those delectable brows. "Don't you think you should have asked me first? What if I had plans?"

"You'd change them because you wouldn't want to disappoint Saralyn." He tried out his innocent look, which usually had the effect of scaring the crap out of people. "So how about it? You said you didn't have any plans, and I need to show the guys that I can score at least one date every year or two."

She laughed. "It's been that long since you managed to get a date?"

He shrugged. "Of course not. But the women in question usually don't hang around long enough to meet the guys. I think it has something to do with my awesome social skills."

"I'm sure it does." She shook her head. "Let me finish pulling this cylinder head off, and then I'll go get cleaned up for the party. I can't get another gasket until tomorrow. Are you going to come pick me up, or should I meet you there?"

Shotgun grinned. "I knew you'd say yes! I'll just wait here, and take you back with me. That way you won't have a chance to change your mind."

* * *

"So you're the one who's stolen our sharpshooter's heart." Kaeden looked like something right out of a Norse mythology book, complete with the long blond hair tied back with a leather strap. He enveloped her in a bear hug before she had time to avoid it.

"Easy, Sarge. The little girl doesn't like to be mauled by strangers." Shotgun managed to extricate her from his buddy's clinch.

Kalie rolled her eyes. "For the umpteenth time, I'm not a little girl."

"Well, you're not very big." The speaker was a lanky man with a mop of dark curly hair. Trace? Or Pete? She was so not good at this friendly group thing. She'd already managed to forget half their names.

"Trust me, if you piss her off she's big enough." Saralyn came to her rescue. "I remember how she used to drive the guards nuts back in the lab. If you're not careful, she just might consider resurrecting some of her nastier tricks."

"Well now, that's a serious threat." The laughter in his eyes betrayed his total lack of concern for her possible retaliation.

"So Shotgun says you've been having some trouble with your car lately. He thought maybe someone might be sabotaging it on purpose?" Right, the guy with the dark hair was Pete. This was Trace.

She nodded slowly. "Yeah. A couple of minor incidents, but I think I've got it under control now." She flashed an irritated look at Shotgun. He'd been talking to his teammates about her. She wasn't sure how she felt about that.

Dee linked her arm through Kalie's and pulled her away from Shotgun's comforting presence. "I'll let you in on some of the guy's weaknesses. We girls need to stick together."

"I'm not so sure that's a good idea." Kaeden grinned indulgently. "Seems to me when you girls get together it's us men that suffer. I remember the tree-hugging incident quite clearly."

"Oh, pooh. You deserved that, and then some. I think you got off lucky that day."

"Lucky?" Shotgun's eyebrow shot skyward "You've got to be kidding."

"Nope. You were definitely lucky." Dee led Kalie over to introduce her to Wren, her little sister.

The evening went well, and Kalie began to relax. She'd never had a family, but she'd always imagined that this is what one would feel like. Happy. Joking with each other. Some good-natured ribbing, but underneath she could sense a bond as strong as any she'd ever seen. These guys really cared about each other, and it showed.

Shotgun had brought her here and made it plain that he cared about her, and they accepted her just like that. He wanted her here, and that was good enough for them. Wow. Just... wow. She'd never expected this kind of acceptance, had never even conceived that it might exist outside of fairy tales. This feeling of belonging, of being accepted just as she was without any conditions or expectations. It was so far from anything she'd ever known, she felt like pinching herself just to make sure she wasn't dreaming.

"You have to come see my garden before it gets too dark." Dee bounced to her feet and beckoned Kalie to follow her.

"Sure." Kalie stood, glancing over at Shotgun. He seemed content to let her go with the other women. She'd never let herself consider settling down. The threat of exposure was too immediate, but all of a sudden she found herself longing for just that. To settle down in one place and be part of a group who really cared about each other. It seemed like an impossible dream.

She followed Dee toward the kitchen, and Saralyn bounced up to tag along.

Dee turned, her hands in constant motion as she talked. "So when I first came back here, the guys were using the yard to dump spare parts and there wasn't anything even remotely green to be found out there. When I told Kaeden I wanted to start a garden he thought I was nuts. No one grows food in the city. I kept nagging though, until he finally decided it would be easier to humor me than to listen to me. I got him to bring in some decent soil from a farm outside the city, and then the guys built me some raised beds and a couple of plant boxes. I got the idea from an old book I found."

Kalie followed Dee out the back door and into another world. Lush vegetation covered every available inch of space. Green and yellow beans, peppers, tomatoes and all sorts of other vegetables hung in various stages of growth from large bushes and vines laden with cucumbers and crisp green peas drooped from trellises that crisscrossed the yard. She'd never seen so much fresh food in one place in her life. She turned to Dee, her mouth open in wonder. "I'm speechless. This is amazing."

"Thanks. I'm really proud of what I've accomplished here." Dee eyed up her little garden. "But that's not why I brought you out here. We wanted to talk to you about Shotgun."

"What about him?" Great. She knew this was too good to be true. They were going to tell her to leave him alone before she brought a whole passel of trouble down on their heads.

"We're trying to be helpful, not scare you off." Dee frowned. "I don't mean to sound like a protective older sister, and I'm pretty sure Shotgun would not appreciate me butting my nose into his business, but he's like a big brother to me."

"To us." Saralyn piped up. "And it's obvious that he's fallen for you hard, which is the point because Shotgun has never taken more than a passing interest in a woman before."

"Which means you could hurt him real bad, and we don't want that." They both shook their heads emphatically.

"The guys have been together a long time, and they have a kind of bond thing going. I swear they communicate by osmosis, and then wonder why we have no idea why we don't know what they are doing." Dee looked at Saralyn, and both of them giggled.

"I kind of noticed they're closer than most guys." Kalie wasn't sure where they were going with this, or why they felt the need to explain it to her.

"Exactly!" Dee looked pleased. "That's what I'm trying to say. The guys have been to hell and back together, and they're more than just a group of mercenaries. If one of them were captured, the others would be all over it before the government had time to tattoo the number on his shoulder. And don't kid yourself. They'd get him or die trying. These guys are joined at the hip. Ain't any of them planning on selling the others out, or leaving them behind. When you bond with one of these guys, you don't just get him. You get them all and they will look after you just like they look after each other, because they know how much we mean to their brothers. I ran out on Kaeden a few years back, and he let me go because he knew I needed the space. But, he kept close tabs on me even if I didn't realize it at the time. As soon as he thought I was in real danger, he and the rest of the guys were right there to haul my ass back to safety. And then they risked their lives to help me get my sister out of trouble, too. That's just the way they are."

"You looked pissed back there when Trace asked you about your car. Like you thought Shotgun shouldn't have talked about you with his buddies. That's the thing, though. He will always share with the other guys. Ask their advice. Just share whatever he knows. Being with one of these guys is not like any other relationship you might get yourself into. You need to consider this carefully." Saralyn looked up at her with a sober expression. "Do you want Shotgun, knowing that he comes with all these attachments? He's never going to walk away from the guys to be with you. If you can't handle that, you need to put a stop to this right now. While you can both still walk away."

Could she walk away, or was it already too late? If you'd asked her just a week ago, she would have assured you that she was tough, and independent, and no guy would ever mean more to her than her freedom.

Now she wasn't sure what she believed. Was that gut-wrenching, soul-searing jolt of pure joy she felt every time Shotgun walked into sight love? Or lust? Or both? How could she tell the difference?

"You finished ogling all the green stuff? It's getting late, and I had an early start this morning." Shotgun stood outlined in the kitchen doorway.

How long had he been there? Had he heard what Dee and Saralyn had been saying? Kalie turned to the other women. "This is really amazing. Thank for showing it to me, and for all the advice. I'll keep it in mind." She hoped her smile wasn't as shaky as it felt.

"No problem." They both smiled at her. Sincere friendly smiles that told her they really were ready to accept her, they just wanted to be upfront about the terms.

And she understood, she really did. If she hurt their friend, they'd come after her like an alley cat protecting its kittens. All claws and sharp teeth.

* * *

They made it back to her place without actually ripping each other's clothes off. There was some groping and pawing involved, but altogether Shotgun was very proud of himself. By mid-point in the drive, his pants felt six sizes too small, and his cock was throbbing with eagerness. Good thing she didn't live any farther away.

Kalie fumbled with the keys for what seemed like an eternity before the door finally swung open and he practically dragged her through it. "Nice place. Love the color scheme."

He had no idea what color the wall was, and he couldn't care less. Backing her up against the wall, he fastened his mouth on hers and allowed himself to feast.

She tasted ripe and so very, very ready. He nibbled on her lower lip, teasing her mouth open to plunder the sweetness within. Leaning into her soft curves, he let her feel the full extent of his arousal. He had a feeling that as long as he was anywhere near Kalie, this was going to be an ongoing problem.

His tongue tangled with hers, and he felt her shudder with pleasure. Despite her tough girl attitude, she was an innocent when it came to sex. She had no idea how to disguise her reaction to him, or else she just plain didn't care.

He felt a flare of hot satisfaction at the idea that she hadn't kissed many men before him. Sex was one thing, but kissing was intimate, a connection that he selfishly wanted to keep for himself. He knew it was corny but no woman had ever affected him like this before. He wanted to wrap himself around Kalie and keep her safe, a pretty tall order considering her background.

Without letting her go, he shrugged out of his shirt and reached for hers. He wanted, no needed, to be skin to skin. He needed to bury himself deep inside her, where he belonged, and he didn't want to let go of her for even a second.

He savored the taste of her, forcing himself to take it slow, show her he could be tender. Their first encounter had been on the tailgate of a truck, and although he didn't regret making love to her so soon after meeting, he regretted the setting. He wanted her to think of him as an amazing lover, someone who would make every encounter a magical experience. A quickie on a tailgate was hardly the impression he wanted her to remember. So, tonight he needed to change that. After tonight, when she looked at him he wanted her to see something different, someone different. Someone she couldn't bear to be without.

They were both naked now, and he swept her up in his arms. "The bedroom?" He didn't want to waste the time looking for it.

"Down the hall." She pointed the direction with her head as she wrapped her arms around his neck.

He reclaimed possession of her mouth, and a breathy little moan escaped her throat. His cock swelled to almost painful proportions. He'd never felt this way with any other woman, this amazing combination of out-of-control lust and the urge to be gentle at the same time.

He laid her on the bed, and she watched through half-closed eyes as he straddled her hips. Reaching forward, he explored her body, mapping her curves with the palms of his hands. He took his time, enjoying every moan, every sharp intake of breath, every indication that she felt this as much as he did.

He didn't rush her, teasing her breasts with his tongue and teeth until she squirmed helplessly beneath him. When she tried to reach for him, he captured her wrists in one hand and drew them up over her head. "Not yet. This time it's all about you. I want you so hot you're begging me."

She opened her eyes wide, locking them on his face. The pupils were so large they almost wiped out the rest of her eyes. "Please. Shotgun. I can't take it anymore." She caught her lower lip in her teeth, and he'd never seen anything so damn sexy in his entire life. Desire swept through him, so intense he couldn't wait any longer.

Bracing himself above her, he nudged her thighs apart and positioned himself at the entrance to her sex. Already, he could feel the moisture gathering. She was ready. "Damn, you are so beautiful." He thrust hard, seating himself balls-deep in her warm channel. She closed around him, her slick warmth gripping him and welcoming him deep inside her.

He managed to hang onto his sanity for a few more precious seconds. He pulled himself almost all the way out, then slid back in with excruciating slowness. Kalie let out a low whimper and wrapped her legs around his waist.

That simple movement was his undoing. He couldn't hold back any longer. Lust roiled through him as he pumped in and out of her exquisitely tight sex. She met him thrust for thrust, unintelligible sounds issuing from her throat as they roared toward a shared climax. The sensations rocketed through him and he let out a yell of sheer male triumph as his orgasm burst over him. Her sex clamped down on him, milking his seed in long slow waves that left him breathless.

If this is what love felt like, he never wanted it to stop.

Chapter Four

"It's almost start time. I need to get into position." Kalie reached up to give Shotgun a quick peck on the cheek. Somehow, having his solid presence at her side had a settling influence on those damn butterflies that multiplied in her belly as race time drew near.

"You need a better kiss than that. For good luck." Tilting her head up, Shotgun wrapped his arms around her and seared a kiss across her lips, letting his mouth linger for an endless minute on hers. She let herself luxuriate in it for a moment, luxuriate in the almost unfathomable fact that this great big hunk of man had nothing better to do than stand here and help settle those dang butterflies.

"Go get them, little girl. I'll be waiting right here at the finish line when you're done showing those yahoos how a car should be driven." He slid his hands down her arms in a soft caress before he finally let her go.

She was starting to like being called little girl. Did that make her weird? Firmly ignoring the butterflies that felt like they were multiplying by the hundreds inside her belly, Kalie secured her helmet and slid into the cockpit of her car. Making sure the safety harness was secured seemed to help settle the butterflies down a bit. At least if she made a major mistake, she'd probably live to tell her grandchildren about it.

Wow, where had that come from? She'd never ever considered having children before Shotgun showed up. The guy was a damn bad influence on her. She felt a soft smile start to curve the corner of her mouth. Be a scary bunch of kids with them for parents.

Taking a deep breath, she started the engine. As it revved up, she let her senses flare out. She immediately felt that almost magical connection to the machine, the legacy of all the horrors in the lab. Not everything from that period in her life turned out bad. Her consciousness expanded to explore every nook and cranny of the mechanical wonder, checking for anything that felt off.

Nothing.

The car was behaving perfectly; every little bit of metal doing exactly what it had been designed to do. Shotgun was probably right -- there was nothing wrong. She was letting her nerves and her imagination see problems where they didn't exist. Not surprising, given the huge changes in her life lately and how much was riding on this race.

She glanced at her watch. Five minutes to the start of the race. She blew a kiss at Shotgun, fully aware that he couldn't see the gesture from inside the helmet. The drive to the start line gave her time to warm the car up, accelerating fast and then braking hard. Her tires needed to be warm, and the engine running at peak in order to get away from the start line clean. A good start would be essential to placing in the race.

She glanced at the other cars. A total of twenty drivers had been invited to participate and she'd lucked out, drawing the inside forward position for start.

The starter signalled the last warning, and Kalie watched a couple of mechanics scramble away from the cars. She wondered idly what it would be like to have to depend on someone else to tell her if her car was running properly.

Flexing her fingers on the steering wheel, she eased her car into the favored slot, mentally counting down the last sixty seconds.

The flag dropped, and her focus narrowed to the first critical corner. She needed to get there fast, and she needed to avoid the heavier cars that would jostle for position. There weren't a lot of rules out here, and some of the drivers would target her just because she was female, and because she'd been showing them up for years. This wasn't a popularity contest, and she'd made her share of enemies.

She rounded the first corner in a good position. Two cars had made it ahead of her, but she'd heard the sickening squealing of metal on metal behind her that signified more than one car was already out of the race. She didn't look back.

The course was a loose circuit through the roads on the outskirts of the city. A mixture of corners, long straight stretches and engine-testing hills ensured that the cars would have a good workout. After the first corner, the cars started to spread out, which suited her just fine. She planned to hang back just behind the leaders until just before the end. As long as she didn't lag too far, she'd be able to swing to the outside and blast past the lead cars before they knew what hit them.

She let her senses expand, keeping a close feel on how the car was running. That was the one wildcard here. Her ride had to be running at peak in order to pull this off. So far, so good.

* * *

The truck came out of nowhere. One moment, she was cruising along with seven car lengths between her and anyone else on the road, the next this behemoth of a truck on steroids was right beside her. With the roughest part of the race just around the corner, the last thing she wanted was to compete for space on the blacktop with something that outweighed her by a factor of three.

Damn.

This was what she got for concentrating too much on the car, and not the other drivers. Dropping a gear, she slammed her foot down on the throttle and brake. The engine screeched as the car shed speed and fell back.

The truck-from-hell must have been anticipating that move, though, and matched her. There went the theory that it was just a coincidence. It started to move sideways, trapping her between its bulk and a high cement block wall. Not a place she wanted to be.

He'd expect her to try to outrun him, and it might even work. While the truck had bulk in its favor, her vehicle was lighter and faster. The question was could she get clear of him before he smeared her all over this wall?

Maybe. If she managed to outwit him first.

Instead of accelerating, she took a deep breath and repeated the braking maneuver. This time, she managed to drop a full car length behind the truck before the driver reacted. And while he braked to get back into squishing position, she jerked hard on the steering wheel and got herself into the outside lane. Calling on every bit of horsepower under the shiny blue hood, she accelerated sharply. She needed to get the hell out of here.

The corner came up fast, and she had to do some pretty slick juggling to stop her ride from sliding off the blacktop. She didn't have time to check on the whereabouts of the truck, or anyone else. When the car quit its bucking and sashaying, she breathed in a deep sigh of relief. It was short-lived.

The black truck roared up behind her, bumping her hard. Shit! She dropped a gear and tramped on the gas, a sinking feeling in the pit of her stomach. She couldn't possibly manage to outmuscle the damn thing, and it looked like he could match her ride for speed as well

Sure enough, black filled her rearview mirror again as her car rocked from another direct impact. How many more of those would she be able to take? At least the car was behaving this time. She let herself merge with it, looking for any signs of weakness. Nothing. At least that wasn't an issue, but she certainly hadn't reinforced the outside structure. This wasn't supposed to be a demolition derby.

A car appeared up ahead of her. There might be safety in numbers. She sure as hell hoped so. Bracing herself for the next impact, she concentrated on pouring everything she had into catching up with the leaders.

The next hit came out of the blue. Instead of ramming her bumper from directly behind, the truck swung wide and hit the right rear panel.

For a single split second, she could see the driver's face. Rage contorted his features, but the eyes were what sent a chill down her spine. This was personal. He wanted to hurt her. And she had no idea why. Or who the hell he was.

The off-center impact had her reeling, her forward momentum sending her into a complete spin before she managed to get the vehicle under control. Shit. Shit. Shit.

This guy really meant business. What the hell? She no longer cared about the race, she just wanted to cross the finish line alive.

She glanced around wildly, hoping to spot an alley too narrow for the other vehicle to follow her. No such luck. This end of town didn't sport those handy little things. Too bad.

The truck hung behind her for a full mile. Taunting. Letting the tension build. That glimpse of the driver's face haunted her, but she shook it off. Right now who and why was so less important than getting out of this alive.

If she could just hang in for another five miles…

The hit was calculated to take her out of the race. Permanently. Every hit leading up to this had been a game.

Cat and mouse. The memory of a cat, playing endlessly with its victim before ending its life with a simple toss in the air, snapping the little neck with casual disregard, went through her mind. Same game. Hopefully not the same results.

Time slowed. The car spun. Endlessly. Kalie squeezed her eyes shut. Willed her stomach to stay put. Thank God there was no cliff edge here. No solid walls to crash into. She slammed the shifter into neutral, letting the car go where it needed to until the revolutions slowed.

The final hit she expected, the end game, never materialized.

The car slid to a halt. She opened her eyes, blinking to clear her vision.

When she finally managed to focus, she saw three trucks. Her nemesis, the black behemoth, stood with its doors open. The other two were easier to recognize. Relief flooded her. Shotgun's ride stood guard on one side of the black truck, while the mercenary group's jeep crowded close on the other side. The driver of the black truck stood defiantly in the middle of the group of ex-soldiers, his hands up in a defensive position.

Kalie watched as Shotgun stalked into the circle, rage showing in every line of his muscular body. He didn't say a word, didn't hesitate. Bringing his fists up, he hammered the other man with a series of quick jabs before sending him staggering with a roundhouse punch to the side of the head.

Seriously? If anyone got to beat the crap out of this guy, it should be her. Opening the door, she leaned against the car for a moment as a wave of dizziness swept over her. Okay. Maybe not up to beating the crap out of anyone at the moment, but she at least wanted to know why. She was positive she'd never seen that guy before.

"Kalie. You okay?" Trace left the circle to come to her side.

She shook off his helping hand. The last thing she wanted was to appear weak in front of an enemy. And know him or not, it appeared she had one very determined enemy. "I'm fine. And I want to talk to that asshole before Shotgun kills him."

Trace grinned, relief in his eyes. He raised his voice. "Hey, Shotgun, your lady would like a word with your punching bag."

Shotgun slowed. Turned. Looked straight at her. The relief in his eyes was palatable. "Kalie."

Her name. That's all he said but it resonated through her, deep down inside her, and she knew. Just like that, she knew she loved him. She could feel the smile blossoming on her face. She tried to focus her energy on the issue at hand but it was hard. "Hey, babe. I want some answers before you finish up here."

Shotgun turned and grabbed the swaying man by the arm. "No problem. I'm sure I can convince my buddy here to cooperate. What did you want to know?"

The circle parted to let Kalie through. She needed to remember to thank them later, for being here for her. She wasn't sure how they'd managed to materialize out of thin air, and she didn't really care. She was just glad they had.

She stepped to Shotgun's side before addressing the stranger. "Who are you? And why did you try to run me off the road? Is winning the race really worth that much to you, that you'd practically kill me to do it? I wasn't even one of the lead cars!"

The man spat in the dirt at her feet, earning himself a sharp cuff across the side of the head from Shotgun. He ignored the mercenary, lips curled in contempt as he addressed her. "My name's Grogan, but that's not important. You're one of those. An abomination. You're not human, and yet you prance around like you think you can fool us." He tossed his head. "These guys have any idea what you are, little lab rat? Do they know what they're putting themselves on the line for? You don't recognize me, do you?"

Kalie shook her head, slowly. No matter how hard she tried, he just didn't look familiar. "Do I know you?"

He snorted. "You don't have to. I know you. I was there when they strapped you down to that table and connected the wires. I know you are an abomination, just like the rest of them and you need to be exterminated. When sabotaging your car didn't work, I decided to take a more direct approach."

Shotgun twisted the guy's arm, forcing him to his knees. Pulling a Glock out of the waistband of his pants, he held it to the man's temple. "I've heard enough. Kalie?"

She shook her head. How could some people hate so much? She'd done nothing to this man, other than be unlucky enough to be tortured in his presence when she was a kid. She looked the man in the eye for a long moment. He stared right back, his eyes narrowed in fanatical hatred. She wasn't a person to him, she was an animal that he intended to kill, but she'd be damned if she'd lower herself to his level. And, she didn't want Shotgun to have this man's death on his hands just because he had been unfortunate enough to meet her. He'd had no idea what he was getting himself into, and she felt a tiny bit guilty about that. Not guilty enough to let him go, however.

Moving to his side, she smiled sweetly. "I don't want you to kill someone on my behalf. Can't we just rough him up a bit and send him on his way?"

Shotgun put an arm around her waist, returning her smile with an evil grin. "I think that can be arranged." He turned to Kaeden, lifting one eyebrow. "Sarge?"

The blond Viking nodded curtly. "We'll take care of it. You just make sure your woman is okay."

"Thanks." Shotgun relaxed ever so slightly, pulling her closer to him, and Grogan took the opportunity to make a grab for the gun.

Shotgun didn't hesitate. Turning his body to shield Kalie, he flipped the gun around and clipped the man across the side of his head with the butt of the pistol. Grogan crumpled to the ground with a meaty thud.

"Just had to, didn't you?" Kaeden strode forward to stand over the prone figure. "Now we're going to have to make sure he knows he's not welcome to come back. It would have been simpler if you'd just shot him."

"Yeah." Shotgun prodded Grogan with one foot. "But a head shot is so messy, and then we'd have to explain all that blood."

"True." Kaeden grinned at Kalie. "Practical guy, this boyfriend of yours. You two might want to go take care of Kalie's car while we make this cutie pie disappear." His grin became less friendly. "Don't worry. He won't be bothering you again."

* * *

"So what do you suppose they did to Grogan?" Kalie hooked her arms around Shotgun's neck.

"Whatever they do, it's not going to be bad enough." He leaned down to taste the sweetness of her lips. "He tried to kill you."

"But killing him isn't the answer." She smiled softly. "He isn't worth it, and I'm much too happy right now to wish anyone harm, even an idiot like Grogan."

"Really?" He nibbled his way from the corner of her mouth to the tender spot right behind her ear lobe. "Because I think I would be okay with knowing he was absolutely positively never going to have another chance to harm you."

"Well, he's not, because you and Kaeden and Trace and all the rest of them are going to make sure that I'm safe." She giggled as he teased her neck with his tongue. "Now there's only one thing standing in the way of our eternal happiness."

He quirked an eyebrow. "And that would be?"

She suppressed an evil laugh. "I don't know your real name. How can I be in love with you if I don't know your name?"

He shook his head. "No one's called me anything but Shotgun since boot camp."

"Not good enough." She ducked her head to avoid another kiss. "Cough it up. What's your real name?"

He sighed heavily, shaking his head in mock concern. "Promise you won't leave me?"

She nodded. "How bad could it be?"

He let out another heavy sigh. "It's bad…"

She waved one hand in the air. "Come on. Tell me."

"Oliver."

She felt her eyebrows rise sharply. "Seriously? Your name is Oliver?"

He nodded.

She crinkled her nose. "I think I'll just call you Shotgun."

He lowered his head to give her mouth a thorough kissing. "Good plan. Now let's see how long it takes me to get you out of those pants."

"Oh, I don't think that's going to take long." Kalie reached down to unsnap the catch at the waist of her jeans. "Not long at all!"

Winter's Quest (Mercenaries 4)

Anne Kane

Winter remembers all about the insanity of life as a lab rat, but what she doesn't know is how she got there. Given the mess she's made out of her life up to this point, she needs to find the answers to her past before she can get on with her future.

Trace isn't sure why Winter is so hung up on her past but if she plans on chasing all over the nine provinces looking for answers then it's up to him to make sure she stays safe. And, while they're spending all that quality time together, maybe he can convince her that he's more than just a convenient sex partner.

Chapter One

Two weeks prior

"Hey, soldier boy. Want a drink?" Winter tossed a can of beer at the big mercenary they called Trace. She'd been watching him for a while now, admiring the way he moved and the way his tight shirt clung to his massive chest when he stood still.

A lot to admire in that package. She wet her lips with the tip of her tongue. Definitely a lot to admire. She'd been celibate much too long.

Trace plucked the can out of mid-air as if he were used to having things tossed in his direction in the dim light of a bonfire. "Thanks. Don't mind if I do." Popping the tab, he took a long pull on the brew, his eyes appraising her with a disarming frankness. "So, you come here often?"

Winter burst out laughing. He certainly was direct. "Is that the best pickup line you've got?"

The big mercenary grinned, taking a seat on one of the many old stumps scattered around the fire. "I'm not much of a ladies' man. My pickup lines are all a bit rough."

"I'm not much of a lady so I guess that makes us about even." Winter grabbed another beer and made her way over to sit on a stump beside Trace.

Now that Saralyn and Brice had decided to introduce a group of mercenaries into their midst, she realized how just how long she'd been celibate. Hiding secrets had a way of discouraging much in the way of intimacy, and her suspicious nature didn't help either.

One look at Trace had rekindled familiar warmth in her gut, though. *Lust. Need. Want.* It didn't really matter what kind of label you put on it, there was only one way to defuse the heat building deep inside her.

The only decision she needed to make was whether she made the first move, or sat demurely waiting for Trace to notice her.

Patience wasn't her strong suit.

Opening her beer, she tipped her head back and took a healthy swig. "So, Brice says you guys are a standup bunch, don't side with the Alliance much."

Trace shrugged. "The Military Alliance doesn't hold any attraction for guys like us. We were on the wrong side of the Provincial wars, and most of us lost everything we cared about either during the wars, or afterward when the Alliance took over. Kind of took all the fun out of things. Nowadays, we only take on contracts we feel are worth fighting for. We make enough to survive on, and not much else but that's okay. We don't need a lot and we watch each other's back. Kind of like what you gals do for each other."

So he knew about her and her sisters. They weren't blood relatives. They were much closer than that. They'd been to hell and back together, and they didn't plan on making a return trip.

"You got a girl waiting for you to come home tonight?"

He raised one brow. "Not very subtle, are you?"

She shrugged. "I don't hunt in another woman's forest."

"And you plan on doing some hunting tonight?"

She gave him her most seductive smile. "Already have. Just haven't closed on in for the kill shot yet. I'm waiting to see if there's a brand on the critter."

His blue eyes twinkled with a mixture of laughter and lust. "Can't say as any woman's bothered to lay claim to me. Yet."

"Well then." Winter stood and held out her hand. "Can I interest you in a private tour of a lovely clearing in the forest? It features a soft mossy floor and enough privacy for whatever strikes our fancy."

Trace took the offered hand. "Love to. I don't get to see a lot of clearings in my line of work. I'll just need to let the Sarge know I'm going to pull a disappearing act. He's a bit of a worrywart, you know?"

She nodded. "The best leaders are. I'll tip off a couple of my sisters, and meet you at the North edge of the pit."

Trace nodded, and pulled her in close. Lowering his head, he seared a kiss across her lips that scorched her to the very core. Damn. Either she was way more desperate than she'd realized, or he was one talented kisser. Maybe a bit of both?

Trace raised her hand to his lips, teasing the center of her palm with the tip of his tongue. Waggling his eyebrows he gave her the sexiest grin she'd ever seen. "I can't wait to see your little clearing."

* * *

"So what do you think?" Winter swept her arm in a wide arc to encompass the entire clearing.

Trace gave the forest glade the briefest of glances. "It's everything you said, but not nearly as lovely as the woman at my side."

Pulling her into his embrace, he reclaimed her lips, giving her the kind of kiss a man gives a woman when he intends to make sure she is supremely satisfied with him. It involved lips and tongue and a lot of passion. He might not be the most cultured guy around but he did what he did with enthusiasm.

Winter surprised him by taking over the kiss, winding her arms around his neck and sliding her tongue along the side of his in an erotic duel that set his blood on fire. She kissed him with a fierce intensity that took his breath away. He'd never met a woman so honest about her sexuality before, one who was comfortable making the first move and asking for what she wanted. He felt a strange sense of connection to her, had since he'd first seen her earlier this evening. There was something about the way she carried herself, the self-confident way she strode amongst her sisters, that touched a chord somewhere deep inside him.

Hell, maybe he had a heart after all. Wouldn't that surprise the guys!

He felt her hands go to the waist of his jeans, fumbling with the buckle on his belt, and he suddenly found it hard to think about much of anything except how very much he wanted the woman in his arms.

Winter made short work of both the belt and the fastenings on his jeans, and then her fingers touched his shaft, exploring the length before pulling it free of his underwear and cupping his balls.

Damn, she definitely wasn't shy.

He pushed her shirt up, not surprised to find that she didn't wear a bra. Her breasts were small and pert, the nipples tilted up to the sky. They fit in his hands just perfectly, and the feel of her naked skin against his palms sent a curl of lustful heat right through him.

She let go of him long enough to pull the shirt over her head and throw it carelessly to the ground, and he took advantage of the time to rid himself of the rest of his clothes. He didn't intend this to be one of those hurried encounters where both participants kept half their clothing on in anticipation of a quick departure. Hell no. When he was done with Winter she wouldn't forget him come morning.

Winter sucked in an audible breath as the metal zipper on his pants clanked noisily against a rock on the ground. Her gaze locked on his groin and he felt himself grow even larger under her eager scrutiny.

"Damn, you are one fine specimen of a man." A single step brought her to his side and then she was touching him everywhere. His chest. His hips. His buttocks. She wrapped her thumb and forefinger around his cock and traced its length.

Trace let out a breath he hadn't been aware of holding. He wasn't going to last long if she kept this up. Grasping her hands, he pulled them up to rest on his chest, while he lowered his head to suck in one delightfully pink nipple. Scooping her up in his arms, he laid her gently on the moss-covered ground.

The earthy damp moss and rocks vied with Winter's unique scent to tease Trace's highly developed sense of smell. He inhaled deeply, his eyes closed as he stored her scent away for future reference. One of the upsides to all the experimental DNA spliced into his was an almost canine ability to recognize people by smell. He'd know Winter anywhere.

She shivered delicately in his arms. She felt small in his embrace, small and very curvy. Whether she wanted to admit it or not, Winter was all woman.

"Trace?" Her voice came out a husky whisper.

"Yeah?"

"You going to just lay there all night or are you going to make love to me?"

He felt a hint of a smile curve his lips, and he lowered his head with slow deliberation until his lips hovered right beside her ear.

"I'm going to make love to you until you beg me to stop, darling, and then I'm going to make love to some more."

"Good." She wrapped her arms around him, scoring her fingernails down his back in a slow sensuous tease. "'Because right now I need me some loving real bad."

Trace slid his hand down across her belly to cup her mound. He could feel the wet heat emanating from her sex. She was ready for him, more than ready. Shifting positions, he straddled her hips, resting his weight on his forearms. Reaching down between them, he parted the soft folds guarding the entrance to her sex and positioned himself to enter.

Brushing the hair away from her face, he stared down into her gorgeous eyes. They were the color of new leaves on a tree in the spring, and right now they were glazed with lust. He felt so incredibly powerful and yet at the same time so very humble. She didn't even know him, but here she lay trembling beneath him, trusting him with her very being. "I have no idea what I did to deserve you, but I'm thankful to whatever quirk of fate led you to me tonight. You are so beautiful."

He kept his gaze locked on her and gave one powerful thrust of his hips, burying himself balls deep in her slick heat. Her tight sheath surrounded him immediately, gripping him, making him feel welcome. "I intend to make you so happy you'll keep coming back for more."

A mischievous twinkle shone through the heat in her eyes. "Give it your best shot, mercenary."

Heat flared through him, dark and edgy. He'd never felt like this before with any female -- this burning lust, this aching desire. He rotated his hips, grinding himself deeper inside her delicious warmth. "You got it, darling!"

"You're so damn big," she whispered softly. "I can feel every inch of that cock of yours."

"It's all for you." Trace circled his hips in a slow tease. Lust flared along every nerve, building up speed as erotic heat gathered deep inside him, urging him to move ever faster. He gritted his teeth, forcing himself to slow down. He wanted this first time to be one of many, and rushing it wasn't going to help his case.

Winter matched him thrust for thrust, her inner walls gripping at him with every stroke. She let out a choked scream, signaling the start of her orgasm. Her sex clamped down hard on his shaft, and he thrust one last time as his own orgasm swept over him, carrying him along in a tidal wave of feeling more intense than anything he'd ever experienced.

Rolling to his side, he collapsed beside her, too spent to hold himself up. He wrapped his warm arms around her, holding her close. She murmured softly, but he couldn't make out the words. It didn't matter. She sounded satisfied.

He didn't know how to describe how he felt about Winter. It had been a long time since he'd bothered to care if he'd satisfied his partner.

Of course, once she learned the truth about him, she'd probably run screaming for the city guards.

Chapter Two

Present Day

Trace watched the way Kalie leaned into Shotgun, as if she could actually draw tangible support from physical contact with the big sniper. A sharp pang of jealousy pierced him. He wanted that. Wanted a woman to lean into him like he was the very center of her existence. If he were totally honest with himself, he wanted Winter to look at him the way Kalie looked at Shotgun, as if he were the center of her universe.

Unfortunately for him, he was too damaged, too warped by the animal DNA the Government had spliced into his own to ever find that kind of acceptance from a woman.

"We really need your help to find her." Kalie's voice quivered just enough to tug at his heartstrings. She really cared about her adopted sister.

"Please." Shotgun gave him one of those brother-in-arms looks guaranteed to make him feel guilty if he even considered saying no.

Trace let out an audible sigh. "So tell me the whole story. I met Winter at that pit party you dragged us to." He had no intention of relating the details of that meeting. "She looked quite capable of taking care of herself, so why are you worried about her dropping out of sight for a day or two? Maybe she met some guy and is shacked up with him across the city. Maybe she's having too much fun and doesn't want to be found." He felt his heart contract at the thought of Winter letting some other guy touch her, laugh with her, make love to her.

Kalie shook her head. "Winter would never do that. None of my sister friends would just leave without telling us where she was going. She's in trouble, and we need to find her." She reached into her pocket and pulled out one of the wrist-mounted com-devices that Jackson had fashioned for them all. "She took this off. Why would she do that if she were just going away for a day or two? Something is very wrong." She let the device dangle from one finger as she chewed on her bottom lip, looking down so that she didn't have to meet his gaze.

Ah, there was more. Trace waited patiently for her to decide to tell him the rest of the story. Kalie might be the love of Shotgun's life, but she was a terrible liar.

Shotgun gently rubbed her shoulders and Kalie growled impatiently. "Fine. She did leave without telling us, which probably means she doesn't want us to find her, especially since she left her com unit behind, but that doesn't mean she isn't in trouble. Just the opposite, in fact. The only reason she'd leave the com unit behind is because she doesn't want us to find her, and that means she thinks finding her will put us in danger. Something's off. I can just tell. Shotgun says you can track down anybody, especially if you have something of theirs. Please, won't you help us find her? If she really doesn't want us, then we'll back off. I just want to know she's okay."

The concern in her voice was real and Trace felt a rush of adrenaline flood his system. He had a very real interest in making sure Winter didn't disappear forever into some black hole the Alliance conveniently forgot to close.

He'd fallen irrevocably in love with the elusive woman. After a lifetime of meaningless one-night stands, with women he could barely remember the next day, that brief encounter with Winter at the gravel pit had changed his life forever. He could remember not only her name, but every inch of her delightfully sexy body. He'd been keeping an eye on her from a distance ever since. He knew he should leave her alone, let her find someone normal that she could settle down and be happy with, but he couldn't quite bring himself to forget about her.

It would be damned inconvenient if she weren't around for him to stalk.

"Do you have any idea why she left, or where she was going?"

Kalie shook her head. "No idea at all."

"Doesn't really matter." Although the information would have come in handy when he found her. "I need an item that's been close to her, preferably skin close."

"Here. Shotgun said this would work." Kalie thrust out her hand, passing him what looked like a pile of material.

He took it and felt an immediate jolt of recognition. Lingerie. Kalie had just handed him one of the most intimate pieces of Winter's clothing, unaware of what it would convey to him.

He schooled his features to their usual impassive state, doing his best to hide the brief flash of possessiveness he'd felt.

Shotgun lifted one brow, his face dead serious. "So? Do you think you can find her?"

Trace nodded, his mind far away, his senses greedily soaking up the information contained in the fabric. His senses flared out of their own accord, seeking the woman whose persona permeated the thin silken garment.

He knew her. Knew her intimately, and now he'd been given carte blanche to find her. What her friend Kalie didn't know was that when he found her, she'd never get away again. He'd let her go once, kept a discreet distance away so she could have a chance at a normal life without him. He didn't think it would be possible to let her go again.

"Now what do we do?" Kalie looked at him expectantly.

"We?" Trace blinked, the question breaking into his trance. "We don't do anything. I do."

Kalie twisted her neck, frowning up at Shotgun. "What does he mean?"

Shotgun put his hands on her shoulders, rubbing soothingly. "That's how it works. He goes off alone and hopefully when he comes back he has your friend with him. Trust me. If anyone can find Winter, Trace can, but you need to let him do it his way."

Trace stood still, watching as Kalie looked from him to her Shotgun. He could see the struggle going on in her expressive countenance, but eventually he saw the acceptance on her face. She nodded slowly. He could tell she wasn't really happy, but then he didn't really care if he made his buddy's girl happy. All he cared about was finding the woman who'd been haunting his dreams since the moment he'd met her.

Closing his eyes, he blocked everything but Winter from his senses. He drew on the energy trapped in the lingerie and remembered the feel of her in his arms that one night when they'd made love.

She'd called it a one-night stand, but then she didn't know Trace. That night had been anything but a one-night stand.

There! He could sense her presence, faint at first but growing stronger as he concentrated, isolating it from everything else. A slow smile curved his lips.

He had her.

* * *

Winter hunkered down in the corner of the tavern, keeping a wary eye on the rest of the patrons. Being alone wasn't a new experience for her but this was different. For the first time since she'd escaped from the lab she'd cut herself off from her sisters. She couldn't risk the big mercenary she'd slept with that night in the gravel pit finding out about her condition, at least not until she'd decided what she was going to do about it.

"You want something else?" The barmaid barely glanced at her as she headed to the bar. Tips would be a whole lot more forthcoming from the rowdy groups of men on the far side of the room.

"No thank you." Winter gave her a polite smile. Slinging drinks in a dive like this wasn't the easiest way to make a living.

"Okay." The woman glanced at Winter's almost empty mug of ale, a briefly sympathetic look on her face. "The boss doesn't like people to stay if they're not drinking. You might want to nurse that if you don't want to get thrown out in the cold."

"Thanks. I will." Winter pulled her coat tighter around her, shivering at the thought of going back out into the dark night. Soon, but not yet.

The barmaid turned on her heels and headed across the room.

A chill of premonition ran down her spine. *What the hell?* The door opened, and her gaze went automatically to the man who entered.

No! Trace. How could he have possibly found her? She knew his buddies bragged about his ability to track down just about anyone at any time, but she'd been very careful. She'd left no indication of where she was going, in fact, she'd left in the middle of the night without even saying good bye to her sisters, and she'd left that damn com-unit behind despite the fact that she felt naked and vulnerable without it. Amazing how quickly she'd come to rely on the instant connection to all of her sisters.

Trace swung his head in her direction as if he knew exactly where she was, pinning her with a glare from his dark eyes.

Silence reigned as all eyes went to the new arrival. He ignored everyone but Winter, pulling his gloves off as he stalked toward her little corner of the pub.

Conversation resumed, although much quieter than it had been. Seems she wasn't the only one who felt the anger emanating from the big mercenary. He stopped in front of her table, staring down at her without saying a word.

"Hi?" Well what the heck did he expect? Not like she'd invited him to come visit her, far from it. She'd made it very clear she wanted nothing more than a single night with him.

He turned to the barkeeper. "Bring me a pitcher of ale, and something with meat in it." Pulling out the chair opposite her, he plunked himself down. "So you want to tell me what the hell you think you're doing?"

Winter blinked. "I beg your pardon?"

"Why did you just up and disappear without telling any of your sisters where you were going? They're worried about you, you know, and you know why."

Winter felt a brief twinge of guilt. It hadn't occurred to her that they might think the Alliance goons had managed to capture her. She hadn't really thought the whole thing through at all, she'd just realized how badly she'd screwed up and she'd run as far away as she could. She thought she'd done a good job of covering up her tracks but apparently she'd been wrong.

"So how did you manage to find me?"

He shrugged. "It's what I do. Find people. Or things. But mostly people."

Well, so much for the fond illusion that maybe she actually meant something to him. Thank goodness he didn't know what had made her run in the first place. The last thing she needed right now was some bad-assed guy thinking he had any right to decide what she should do. Lying would be necessary to extricate herself from this situation. Luckily that was the one thing she was very good at.

"I just wanted out. I'm tired of running and hiding and worrying about getting caught. I want to live a normal life and that's not possible in an Alliance-run town."

Trace looked around the bar room, his gaze lingering on the unsavory characters swilling down the local brew. "Yeah. This looks like a big improvement. I can see the attraction."

Winter felt a smile tug the corner of her mouth. Damn. The guy had an annoying habit of knowing exactly how to get through the wall of ice she'd erected around herself. "It has its good points."

The bartender reappeared and plunked a jug of beer on the table, slopping the contents over the edge before putting two mugs on the table. Glaring at them as if they somehow were inconveniencing him, he held out his hand. Trace slapped some cred-chips in it, fixing the man with one of his icy glares. "We don't want to be disturbed."

The man pocketed the coins, grunting an unintelligible answer before retreating to his bar. Trace's attention returned to her. "So these good points, are we talking about the ambiance or the cheerful serving staff?"

"Okay. I admit it's a bit of a dive, but the price is right." She sighed. "I meant it. I needed to get out of the city and I honestly didn't think about how it would affect the others so you can just turn around and go back and tell them I'm okay and I'll be in touch when I get myself sorted out. I need time to think."

Trace shook his head. Picking up the tankards one at a time he poured them each a generous glassful of the pale liquid. "Think about what?"

He certainly had a way of getting to the heart of the matter. "Things. My life. What I want to do. I can't spend my whole life hiding in the shadows in some city, afraid of getting caught."

Traced raised his glass and took a long pull on the liquid.

She had to give him credit for not gagging. The swill they served here was hardly up to his usual standards.

He sat his glass down on the table. "Okay. You need time away to think. I can respect that. I'll let the others know you're safe and that we'll be back when you're ready to face them."

We? "What do you mean we? I don't need you to stay with me. I don't *want* you to stay with me. I want to be left alone."

"Not happening."

She couldn't believe she was hearing this. He didn't even try to justify himself. He acted so damned superior, as if he thought he had the right to make decisions concerning her. She could just imagine what he'd do if he knew she was pregnant. Oh why the hell did she have to be so damned fertile? It had been one night, just one glorious night and she'd been too caught up in the moment to remember that birth control rarely worked on freaks like her. Brood mares. That insane doctor had altered her genetics to make it practically impossible for her to have sex without getting pregnant.

She hoped there was a special place in hell reserved for mad scientists who experimented on helpless kids.

Composing her face to what she hoped was icy calm she raised one brow at the big mercenary. "I beg your pardon? I don't recall asking for your permission."

Apparently he didn't scare all that easily.

"You didn't have to. There is no way I'm abandoning you here in this cesspool of human lowlifes. I'll be at your side until you're ready to return to the relative safety of the city."

"But I don't want you to stay at my side!"

He shrugged. "That's too bad because I'm not leaving."

Why hadn't she noticed how annoying he could be before this? "Well, you're not staying with me."

"Oh, I think I am."

"Nope." Pushing herself to her feet, she glared down at him. "You're not. Now finish your drink like a good little mercenary and go home." Spinning on her heel she stalked over to the bar, fixing the unfortunate pub owner with her glare.

"I need a room."

"For two?"

"No!"

"But…"

"Yes, she means for two." Trace circled her waist with an arm as soft and yielding as a band of iron. "I will be staying with her."

"Yes, of course, sir." The innkeeper's voice was annoyingly subservient as he wiped his hands on a rag. "Follow me."

Trace leaned in to whisper in her ear. "Behave." Keeping a firm arm around her waist, he fell into step behind the innkeeper.

For a brief moment, Winter considered stomping her feet and throwing a temper tantrum but she doubted she'd get any sympathy from the other patrons of the bar. They'd probably just consider it a bit of free entertainment. Rolling her eyes, she let herself be herded from the room.

The innkeeper led them upstairs, striding down the hallway to push a door open at the far end. "I hope this will serve. You can bar the door from the inside, and the maid will bring a jug of water and fresh towels in the morning."

"It's fine." Trace passed over a rather generous handful of cred chips.

"Yes, sir." Bobbing his head, the innkeeper retreated from the room.

Winter twisted out of his grasp. "Behave? Seriously? What do I look like, your pet dog?"

"No, if I had a dog it would know exactly what I expected of it at any given time. I wouldn't have to remind it to behave."

If she didn't know better, she'd think that twinkle in his eye was humor. She gave her head a mental shake. Trace didn't do humor. Ever. He was the most serious man she'd ever met. Even in the heat of making love, he'd been dead serious.

The subject of her recent X-rated dreams pulled his outer shirt off over his head and tossed it on the bed. Not exactly a move calculated to make her feel more relaxed. His biceps flexed enticingly beneath the remaining thin layer of material.

Crossing the room, he used the tinderbox on the mantel to start a fire in the brick fireplace, adding sticks from the pile beside it until he had a roaring blaze going. The temperature in the room climbed steadily.

Trace got to his feet and turned to face her. The tight shirt clung lovingly to each and every sculpted muscle of his torso. Maybe it wasn't the flames from those burning logs raising the temperature in here.

He fixed her with a stare that was far from icy. As he stalked across the room toward her, she felt like a deer caught in the headlights of an oncoming vehicle. She knew she should run and yet she couldn't get her legs to move.

Reaching her side, Trace cupped the back of her head in one big hand as his mouth slowly descended to devour her lips in a kiss hotter than the logs spluttering in the fire behind them. She closed her eyes and allowed the magic of his presence to wash over her.

What was it about the big mercenary? It's not like she'd never met a male before, and she'd certainly seen guys both cuter and hotter than the one here in this room with her. Trace's face was rugged and masculine, deep worry lines etched permanently into the rough skin. Faint scars bore silent witness to his violent way of life.

And yet, he was the only man to set her blood to boiling, to make her knees go weak with a single glance, to make her forget that a single night of pleasure could have consequences that would haunt her for the rest of her life.

When she'd seduced Trace she'd forgotten all about the heavily boosted morning after pills one of her sisters had concocted for her. Winter had no idea what chemical concoction they contained, but they allowed her to have a normal sex life despite her ever so fertile body. She just had to swallow one of the little pills within an hour of sex and voila: no consequences.

Trace was the only man who had ever overwhelmed her senses to the point of forgetting all about those consequences. She'd been so sated, so incredibly satisfied that she'd happily fallen asleep in his arms as if she didn't have a care in the world.

When she woke up it was too late. She was on her way to being a mommy.

Chapter Three

She'd always been good at rationalizing what she wanted, and tonight wasn't going to be any different. Since she was already pregnant it couldn't hurt to enjoy another night in his arms, now could it? After all, once the baby got here it was going to be damned difficult to date. For the briefest of moments she considered getting rid of the problem, aborting it, but even the thought of that made her feel slightly ill. She might not have planned this child, but she loved it already, and she secretly hoped it had Trace's eyes, if not his annoying habit of being able to see right through her motives.

He kissed like he did everything else, passionately. His entire attention was devoted to devouring her lips as his mouth blazed across hers. Heat sparked across every inch of her skin. Had pregnancy increased her sex drive, or was it just that she felt free to enjoy every second of this encounter since the damage was already done?

It didn't really matter, and now was so not the time to worry about silly things like motives and consequences. There was no doubt in her mind that they would come crashing down on her later. Right now, she intended to wring every last drop of sensual pleasure that she could out of Trace's willing participation.

She fit against him perfectly, like she'd been born just for him. When she'd looked up and seen him coming through the door down in the common room, she thought he'd looked glad to see her, despite the ice in his eyes. Her heart had done a curious little dance in her chest, hoping in some dumb foolish part of her that he'd come because he couldn't bear to be without her.

Whether she was willing to admit it or not, she wasn't immune to his particular brand of sexy.

"You are so beautiful. Before I met you, I just existed. I had no idea the world could be such a wonderful place." He whispered the words into her ear, as if he were afraid to say them out loud. Maybe she wasn't so crazy after all. Maybe there was a chance for the two of them.

She let out a strangled gasp as he feathered a flurry of tiny kisses down her neck to the tender hollow of her throat. He worshiped her wordlessly for a long moment, his mouth moving over her possessively, hungrily, and lovingly.

What if she were kidding herself? What if he really didn't feel anything at all for her except lust?

He nipped a tiny fold of skin at her throat, sending a shiver of desire spiking across her nerves and she gave up all attempts at rational thought. For tonight, at least, she intended to live in the moment.

Tomorrow would be soon enough to resume worrying about the future.

Scooping her up in his arms, he crossed the room in a single step and tossed her onto the bed before pausing to divest himself of his clothing. He had a magnificent body, one she could happily spend the rest of her life admiring. His cock was already rock hard, jutting proudly up from the tangle of dark hair at his groin. She wet her lips with the tip of her tongue in silent invitation.

Trace moved with deceptive speed. One moment he was standing beside the bed, his cock bobbing enticingly at eye level, the next he was reaching for her with tightly leashed lust.

"Taste me."

He didn't have to ask twice. Winter reached out to grasp his thick shaft in her hand, tracing the thick vein that ran from the base to the tip with one finger. Lowering her head, she took him in her mouth.

He tasted every bit as good as she remembered, slightly musky, salty and oh so very male. She used her tongue to tease him, running it along the sides of his cock as she hollowed her cheeks to suck as much of him as she could into her mouth. She loved the sound of his sudden intake of breath, the feeling of power it gave her to have the very essence of his maleness in her mouth.

Trace buried his fingers in her hair, tugging softly to urge her to take him even deeper. Closing his eyes, he tilted his head back and slowly rocked his hips as she sucked and licked.

Reaching up, Winter gently cupped his sac, kneading it softly. The twin orbs felt warm and heavy in her hands, and she scored her finger along the skin.

Trace let out a low growl and dragged her up to claim her mouth with his own. A devouring urgency flashed through her as his tongue pushed past her lips and claimed the inside of her mouth. It proved impossible to concentrate with his hands roaming possessively over her body, removing her clothing with consummate ease, and she gave up the effort.

This is what she wanted, what she craved, what she had secretly hoped for ever since that first night in his arms. An actual long-term, happily ever after relationship might be out of the question but there was no reason she couldn't have one more night of amazing sex before she slipped away to start a new life. Was there?

A whirlwind of emotion cascaded through her. Trace's scent surrounded her, invading every pore of her body, sending her libido soaring. They tumbled onto the bed, lips still locked together and she found herself staring up at Trace as he straddled her hips, his massive cock pressing into the soft skin of her belly.

She gasped, wriggling her hips and arching up to try and impale herself on the tempting shaft. Damn. She needed that, needed it planted firmly inside her. Now. Right now.

A deliciously dark smile twisting his lips, Trace braced himself above her on his elbows. Locking his gaze on her, he reached down and positioned himself at the entrance to her slick heat.

Winter held her breath, waiting, anticipating. Darts of erotic fire danced along each nerve as she waited for his invasion.

He lifted his hips, then surged into her, burying himself balls deep with one strong thrust of his powerful hips.

Winter let out a wordless scream as his huge cock stretched her slick sex, filling her impossibly full. That felt so incredibly good. Wrapping her legs around his waist, she arched into him, attempting to take him even deeper.

Trace began to move, shafting her with long sure strokes that sent the lust spiraling deep inside her belly. She rocked her hips, matching him stroke for stroke as a blazing heat began to build across every inch of her naked body. Burying her face in the crook of his shoulder, she inhaled his intoxicating scent.

Trace reached down between them, finding the tiny bundle of nerves at the entrance to her sex, scoring his nail over it.

A strangled whimper escaped Winter as the blazing heat of her desire overwhelmed her. She could feel her orgasm starting, swelling from a tiny place deep down inside, growing until it overwhelmed her, rolling over her with the force of a tsunami.

Her sex clamped tight around Trace's shaft, and he reacted by tightening his hold on her, letting out a roar of triumph as his seed spurted deep inside her.

They stayed locked together for what felt like an eternity as wave after wave of aftershocks rolled through Winter, rocking her resolve to not let Trace get under her skin. She'd worry about that later. She'd worry about everything later. Thinking sucked. Right now she just wanted to revel in the feel of Trace's warm, hard body covering hers.

A long time later, Trace shifted position, rolling onto his side without letting go of her. He was pretty good at that, moving without letting go of her. She kind of liked it. He wrapped one arm behind her head and dropped a gentle kiss on her forehead. "Go to sleep. We'll figure this out in the morning."

Seriously? What did he think he was going to figure out? He had no idea what the problem was, and she had no intention of enlightening him. Winter put her head on his shoulder and closed her eyes.

* * *

Winter groaned softly and tried to ignore the sound of china clinking. If she opened her eyes, she'd have to admit she was awake and then the lovely dream in which she and Trace were cavorting in a cozy little cottage in the woods would disappear forever.

"Come on, sleepyhead. Breakfast is here." Trace sounded disgustingly cheerful for this hour of the morning.

Oh great, a morning person. Just what she didn't need. The aroma of strong, freshly brewed coffee wafted through the air, teasing her senses, and she cracked one eye open just enough to see him pouring a hefty cupful of the thick black liquid.

Then again, maybe having a morning person around might not be so bad -- especially if he were willing to fetch her breakfast in bed every day.

She gave her head a mental shake. No. She would not let herself be seduced by the thought of having someone around all the time, especially someone as wonderful as Trace. It wouldn't be fair to him. He might think he was a hard-assed tough guy, but that wouldn't be enough to keep him safe. No. Not doing it.

Keeping the blanket pulled up tight to her chin, Winter sat up in the bed. "Is that for me?"

Trace grinned over his shoulder. "Yup. Coffee, cinnamon rolls, fresh fruit. Never let it be said that Trace McDougal doesn't know how to treat an overnight guest."

"Yeah." She wrinkled her nose, staring at the tray pointedly. "Are you planning on bringing that over here?"

"Of course. Just waiting for you to show some sign of life." He shook his head in mock amazement. "Did you know that you can sleep through the sound of a major brawl in the hallway outside our room?"

She grinned. "Why should I bother to wake up? As long as they stay out in the hall it's not my problem. Hopefully there aren't any slippery pools of blood out there. Are you going to be long with that coffee?"

Trace picked up the tray and carried it over, placing it carefully on the bed between the two of them. Picking up one of the coffee cups, he handed it to her. "Here you go. I wasn't sure if you preferred pastries or fruit for breakfast so I got some of each."

"Some of each is good." Taking a sip of her coffee, Winter braced herself. Last night had been great, but Trace wasn't going to be put off for long. He'd want to know where she was headed and why.

As if he could read her mind, Trace began. "So you left the city where you had the support of all your sisters, not to mention my team, because you like the ambiance out here in the sticks?" He managed to make that sound like a reasonable question.

Winter sighed. "No. I'm not an idiot." She'd decided the best plan would be to give him enough of the truth to satisfy his sense of rightness without telling him everything. "I want to see if I can find my mother, or any of my family. I had Saralyn hack into the government files and she came up with a name. Not much to go on, but I know where I was originally picked up from so I have to try. I want to know where I come from, who my parents were, if I have any real family left."

Trace shook his head. "I understand wanting to know who you are, but the chances of finding your mother after all this time are pretty slim. Do you have any idea how you managed to land in that lab? Did she sell you? Did someone snatch you for the money? Is she even still alive?"

Winter held out her hands. "Stop it! I know. Chances are she's dead, probably was dead before I even got picked up but I need to know." She paused, trying to find the words to explain the deep-rooted need to understand where she came from. "Maybe I have some other relatives living, maybe not, but I have to try." She realized this would make a whole lot more sense to him if she told him about her own impending motherhood, but that was one secret she planned to keep. "I have to at least try."

Trace looked doubtful. "Okay. So where are we talking about? Surely you don't expect to find your roots in this dive?"

This was where the conversation got a little dicey. "Two provinces over. That's why I'm here. I was supposed to be meeting a guy who could get me a counterfeit pass, but I'm guessing your presence scared him off." She gave him her best innocent look. "I don't suppose you'd happen to have a pass or two in that pack of yours?"

A ghost of a smile crossed his rugged face. "No. That's Jackson's specialty. I need some lead time if you want stuff like that."

Good point. She might have considered that before she took off except that would have nixed the whole sneak away while no one is looking angle. Maybe having Trace along wouldn't be such a bad thing after all. And as a bonus, she wouldn't have to give him up just yet. "You think he could get us a couple of passes? I mean, if you're going to shadow me anyway you might as well be useful."

Trace's brow shot skyward. "Shadow you? I was kind of thinking of tossing you over my shoulder and dragging you back home."

"But you're not going to do that because you're really a nice guy. Right?" She put just a tiny bit of pout into that statement.

He shook his head ruefully. "You are a little minx, you know that? How about I give Jackson a call and see about those passes. We're going to need a cover story to get past the guards at the border. Any ideas?"

She studied one of the cinnamon buns much more seriously than it deserved. "My original cover story was that I was going home to attend a funeral.

We could still use that one if you want, but we'll have to tweak it a bit."

He must have heard the suppressed laughter in her voice. The look on his face was cautious, if anything. "And whose funeral would that have been?"

She peeked up at him from beneath her lashes. "Yours?"

He let out a bellow of laughter. "I don't think that's going to wash. You're going to be traveling as my bond-mate, just to simplify things. We'll be attending my brother's funeral. Much more believable."

Winter took a mouthful of coffee. He really did know how to make a good coffee. "Why is that more believable?"

"Because one look at me, and they'll assume my brother is some kind of soldier. Soldiers die. It's a fact of life. No questions asked, they'll feel sympathy for a fellow soldier and let us through with minimal fuss."

He was right. She knew he was, but still, that didn't stop her from being annoyed. She refused to acknowledge the hard knot that coalesced in the pit of her stomach at the matter-of-fact way he'd said "soldiers die." He was a soldier and the thought of him being shot or knifed or hurt in any way was totally unacceptable. It took a lot of effort to summon the smallest of smiles. "Okay, we'll go with your story."

He nodded, suddenly looking all businesslike. "Good. I'll get Jackson to get the paperwork ready. We can go back and pick it up along with the jeep. No point in humping it on foot across two provinces." He fiddled with the com device on his wrist for a few moments. Winter nibbled on her cinnamon bun and watched him.

He looked so darn competent, and she wasn't sure she liked that. Somehow he'd managed to take charge of her little excursion, delegating her to the status of tagalong. Not that she didn't appreciate his help. It would make the trip so much easier but since she hadn't told him the whole truth, it could turn out to be… interesting. Yes, interesting was the word she was looking for.

If she timed it right, she'd never have to admit to the rest of it.

Chapter Four

"Thanks, Sarge." Trace took the packet of paperwork from Kaeden and slipped it into his back pocket. "Appreciate the help."

"I know we asked you to find Winter, but you don't have to go chasing all over the nine provinces with her." Kaeden managed to put just a hint of a question in the statement.

"Actually I do. She'd going to go whether I do or not, and I need to keep her safe."

"Like that, is it?" A knowing smile curved Kaeden's lips.

Trace shrugged. "Yeah. It is."

"Good luck then." Kaeden gave him a friendly slap on the back. "And make sure you call for backup if you need it. We can be there ASAP. Dee would never let me live it down if either of you get hurt."

Trace couldn't resist. "Like that, is it?"

"Damned straight. That woman runs my life, and I've never been happier." Kaeden shook his head. "Hard to remember back when it was only us guys, isn't it?"

"It was grim. I like the new order, and I'll like it even better when I manage to convince Winter I'm the right guy for her."

Kaeden let out a low whistle. "I've seen the way she looks at you. I thought you guys were past that."

"Nope. Not sure what the problem is but I think it has something to do with this trip to look for her roots. Don't worry. I'm not planning on letting her get away."

Winter came bouncing into the room, followed by Dee and Wren. Putting her hand on his arm in an unconsciously intimate gesture, she grinned up at him. "We're all set. Did you get the papers?"

Trace patted his back pocket. "Got them right here."

"Great. I'll go grab my kit and meet you in the garage. We cleared to take the jeep?"

"Make sure you bring it back in one piece!" Kaeden's glare might have been more effective if his eyes weren't clouded with worry. Trace knew he didn't like the members of his team to take off alone.

Slinging his own kit bag over his shoulder, Trace held out his hand to Kaeden. "Wish me luck, Sarge."

Kaeden took his hand and pulled him into a bear hug. "You got it. Now go get that little lady whatever the hell it is she needs to feel whole and safe."

Damn. Kaeden might look like a redneck jerk, but he always seemed to know just what to say to his team. If this thing went south, he and the rest of the team would be right there to bail him and Winter out. Knowing you had someone at your back was one of the nicest feelings in this whole screwed-up post war world. He hiked the kit bag up on his shoulder and turned to follow Winter out to the garage.

The last thing he wanted was for any of the other Mercs to see him looking other than his usual rough and tumble self.

* * *

"Okay, first checkpoint coming up. You ready?" Trace glance over at Winter. She looked so darn cute, sitting in the jeep dressed as a demure life partner. He'd managed to convince her that in order to keep her under his protection, she had to pose as either his wife or his sex slave. She'd chosen wife. *Huh. Go figure.*

She said the costume required to pose as a sex slave would be chilly.

The thought of her in a slave's garb was intriguing but he wasn't sure he'd be able to restrain himself if other guys were ogling her in scanty clothes. Still, he would have been able to claim he had a possessive streak. Lots of guys didn't like other men looking at their women, wife, or slave. No, it was probably better this way. Only he knew what delights were hidden beneath that baggy tunic and pants outfit.

Winter nodded. "I'm ready. It's not exactly rocket science. I just have to keep my mouth shut and look to you as if I'm an idiot if they ask anything. Just like a true Provincial."

Trace snorted. "You'll do fine. Keep your eyes down, look at the floorboards. Makes it look more realistic."

He pulled up to the guard post and brought the jeep to a halt. His timing was impeccable. The guard had just started his supper, and was annoyed at the interruption, although by the smell of it he should be thanking them. He let them go with only a cursory glance at the impeccably forged documents that Kaeden had supplied.

"Well that went well." Winter relaxed, propping one foot up on the dash and reaching into the back seat for a bottle of water. "Want a drink?"

Trace made a show of gagging. "Not that stuff. It'll rot your insides out."

"Water?" Winter crinkled up her nose. "I think you're mixing it up with that rot gut you guys refer to as ale."

"Nope." Trace eased the jeep around a hairpin turn. "Ale is good. Water is bad. You should really give up the water and switch to a good pure ale."

"Like the stuff they served at that pub we stayed at?" She cocked one eyebrow.

She had a point. "Okay, not all ale is created equal, but the stuff the guys packed for us is primo. Once you try it, you'll never go back to water." He made a circle with his thumb and forefinger to emphasize the point.

Winter made a face at him. "Just the same, I think I'll stick with the water. How long is it going to take us to reach the next checkpoint?"

Trace glanced at the navigation panel. "Not long. We're crossing the narrowest part of the province. Maybe two hours. Then another hour to get to Desolation." He grimaced. "What kind of name is that for a city? It's like saying give up before you even start."

Winter shrugged. "No idea. Probably the idea of our illustrious government. If people get too hopeful, they're likely to fight back and they wouldn't want that."

A ghost of a smile lifted the side of Trace's mouth. That was his girl. Heavy on the sarcasm, especially when it came to the assholes who'd used her as a human guinea pig. "Saralyn got you the info you have on your family?"

"Yes. She did her best, but the records are sketchy. I have an 'address of origin' which I assume is my mother, along with a name. Kathleen O'Malley. There was nothing on my father which could mean my mother didn't know who he was, or that he was influential enough to keep any mention of him off the records."

Trace frowned. "Why would he bother to do that?"

"If he's got a position in the government, he wouldn't want his name connected with any of the lost kids. Kind of a career killer, you know?"

He nodded slowly, swerving to avoid a pothole the size of a small tank. "I guess that makes sense, but the first one is probably more likely."

The mischievous smile on her face tempted him to just pull over and kiss her senseless. He managed to resist the urge.

"You're probably right, but it's more fun to think my daddy might be a rich and famous politician." She rolled down the window and rested her arm on the edge of the window well. "If it turns out he's just some random bum it'll be a big letdown."

"Okay, but at least a random bum won't bother to cause you any grief."

"Good point." She held her bottle of water up in a mock toast. "Here's to random bums!"

A companionable silence settled over them, and he found himself reluctant to break it. It wasn't hard to imagine them as an old bonded couple who didn't need to keep up a constant stream of mindless chatter.

The last checkpoint loomed on the horizon, and Trace felt his nerves jump. A long line of traders were lined up to get through the station. It looked like there was a big market event coming up, and the guards were being extra careful about who got through. Or, they could just be shaking the merchants down for bribes to get across. Either way, it meant they were going to have to be careful not to raise suspicions. He really didn't relish the idea of having to fight his way out of here with Winter by his side. Trace reached over and took her hand, giving it a gentle squeeze.

She wanted answers about her past, and although he had no idea why this was suddenly so important to her, he was going to make damn sure she got them.

The line inched forward with the speed of a slug stranded on hot pavement. When the guard finally motioned them to drive forward and hand over their papers, Trace was bored enough he'd almost welcome a problem as a diversion.

The guard had dreadlocks, eyes that reminded him of a snake he'd shot on his last trip through the desert, and the nastiest rash on his neck that Trace had seen outside of a dump zone. He gave their carefully prepared paperwork a disinterested glance.

"Reason for entering my province?"

His province. Wow, the guy sure didn't have an ego problem. "Funeral. My brother."

"How come she's going with you?" He gestured at Winter as if she were some sort of annoying pest. "She your sister?"

"No. She's my wife and I take her pretty much everywhere. She can look after my needs, if you get my drift." He might as well try for the brothers-in-arms thing.

The guard nodded, his gaze a little too interested as he measured Winter up. "You ever consider renting her out?"

Oh crap. This just might turn into a fight after all. "No." He infused that one word with all the ice he could muster. "I'm not a sharing kind of guy."

The guard shrugged, favoring him with a grin that lacked a few teeth. "Hey, no offence. Just asking. The Governor is having a big shindig to celebrate Market Days and he's looking for some females to provide entertainment. Just thought you might be interested in making some easy money."

"Well, thanks, but not this time." Trace didn't like the way the guard's attention kept sliding back to Winter. The sooner they got out of here, the better. He looked pointedly at the papers the guard still held in his hand. "Are we good to go now?"

"Huh?" The guard looked down at the forged documents. "Oh yeah. Sure." He took a step forward to hand back the papers, lowering his voice. "If you change your mind just give me a shout. I'll make it worth your while."

Trace didn't bother to reply, grateful that Winter was still sitting quietly beside him. When they cleared the checkpoint, she gave him a long hard stare, but she was bright enough not to say anything. You could never be too careful. There was always a chance of being overheard by government sympathizers.

The corner of her mouth quivered with suppressed mirth though, and he took that as a good sign.

Chapter Five

"So now what?" Trace waited until they were well inside the border before pulling over. "Did Saralyn manage to pinpoint an exact location or just a broad area?"

"We have the last known address, but it's a couple of decades old. You know how inaccurate the new government databases have turned out to be. It's in the old part of Desolation so I figure if we start there we may not find her but we might find someone who knows her, or can tell us where she went."

The chance of a woman staying in the same place for over two decades was pretty slim but you never knew. Maybe karma would be on their side and the woman was hunkered down in her ancestral home or some other fantasy come true. Then again, people with ancestral homes generally didn't hand over their children to mad scientists.

Trace nodded. "Desolation it is." He slanted a glance up at the sun as it tracked its way across the cloudless sky. "Should be there in time for dinner."

The drive proved to be uneventful, if somewhat hot. This part of the continent consisted mostly of deserts grown out of the massive bombing attacks of the last war. With no cover from the sun, and no large bodies of water to mitigate the temperature it was uncomfortable to say the least. Unfortunately the jeep sported every new tech device Jackson could come up with, but no air conditioning. Just like a man to make sure you could get the latest sports scores, but not to consider basic comforts.

When the town came into sight, they both heaved a sigh of relief. Trace slowed the jeep and looked over at her. "Do you want to stop for a meal first, or go straight to the old town?"

Winter swallowed the lump that had suddenly appeared in her throat. So close to her goal, she suddenly realized she wasn't sure she wanted the answers. What if it turned out her mother was as big a monster as the doctors at the lab? What earthly reason could a mother have for letting her child be used the way she and the other kids in that lab had been used?

Procrastinating wasn't going to help. She needed to know why she'd been abandoned to such a horrific fate. What if she was like her mother? Maybe if the baby cried too much she'd be willing to abandon it, or worse. How could she live with herself if she failed to protect her child?

She jumped as Trace pulled the jeep to the side of the road and turned to envelop her in his warm arms. Just as suddenly as it had started, the panic receded. She wasn't alone. She had options, and whatever she found in the old town, she could deal with it but she needed to know for the sake of her unborn child.

She buried her head in the crook of his shoulder, taking a deep, ragged breath. She should tell him, it was his child too. Yet another terrifying thought. Did he even like children? How would he react? They weren't exactly a settled old couple, ready to start a family.

"You ready now?"

His gentle voice helped to calm her nerves. She had to do this. More than ever, she needed to know where she came from. She drew in a ragged breath and nodded. "Yeah. Let's do it."

The old part of town looked like any other place that had survived the Provincial Wars. The buildings were still standing, but had the weary look of survivors of a long and vicious battle. Patches of thick mud adorned the sides where bricks had been knocked out, and window glass had been replaced with scarred pieces of Plexiglas. Like so many of the human survivors, the town looked old and tired.

"Turn left at the end of this street." Winter studied the map. "It should be right around that corner."

Trace nodded, reaching out with one hand and placing it on her knee. Without looking at her, without words he let her know he was there for her.

He'd make a great father.

Turning the corner, Trace slowed the jeep as Winter searched for numbers on the old buildings. "We're looking for one seventy-six so it should be on my side." She peered at the grime-covered structures. "There's one twenty-two. Keep going. One forty-eight... one fifty-two... There!" She pointed at a big square old house with a dilapidated porch running the full length of the front. The numbers one seven six were nailed to a board on the fascia, beneath a sign advertising rooms for rent.

Trace pulled the jeep beside the curb and put it in park while he studied the building. "A boarding house."

"Yeah. I guess I just assumed it would be my mom's home."

"It might be. You won't know until you go in and ask. You ready for this?"

She frowned. "You keep asking me that!"

"It seems like a question that needs to be asked a lot."

Winter sighed. "Ready or not, this is something I need to do. Will you come in with me?"

He gave her a look that made her heart feel warm. "Of course. There's no way I'm letting you out of my sight until we're safely back in our own province." Flipping his door open he strode around to her side of the jeep, and held out a hand to help her out. "Let's go slay this dragon together."

She raised her brows. "Slay this dragon? We're going to potentially meet the woman who gave birth to me."

"Which could make her less than happy with the man who is currently bedding her long-lost daughter. I know I wouldn't be happy with some mercenary bedding down with a daughter of mine. Might even make me as scary as a mythical dragon."

"You don't have a daughter?" She realized that sounded like a question. Maybe he had kids running around all over the planet, and didn't care about them. Why hadn't she thought of that before now?

He shook his head. "I don't have a daughter, or a son for that matter, but if I did I'd be willing to kill anyone who laid a hand on them. So, I assume a woman who gave birth to a beautiful girl like you would be willing to do the same."

Winter felt an invisible weight lift from her heart. He'd be an awesome dad! "Don't worry. I'll tell her I seduced you. You didn't stand a chance."

"Thanks. I feel so much better now, especially since that's the truth. One look from those gorgeous eyes of yours and I just had to do whatever you told me to."

Winter snorted, remembering the way he'd taken charge when he'd found her at the inn yesterday. "Not exactly how I remember it, but I'll play along. Shall we?"

They walked up the front path hand in hand and climbed the steps to the porch. Trace reached up and rang the doorbell.

The doorbell echoed loud enough to hear outside, and within minutes a spry elderly lady peered suspiciously out the door at them. "You two looking to rent a room? I don't do by the day so if you're looking to hook up you can go find a hotel."

"Hook up?" Winter frowned. "No, we're looking for a woman who used to live at this address."

"Lots of women used to live here. Got a name?"

"Kathleen. Kathleen O'Malley. She lived her about two decades ago."

The woman stared at her, an odd look on her face. Finally, she spoke. "Yeah. I remember Kathie. What's your interest in her?"

Winter swallowed the lump in her throat. "I think..." This was so much harder than she'd imagined, but she had no choice. "I think she's my mother."

The old woman's eyes widened. "You're alive! She always said you were. You're Winter, right?"

"I am. She did? Is she here?"

The woman shook her head sadly. "You'd better come in. We need to talk. I'm Greta, by the way. Nice to finally meet you." Unlocking the door, she motioned them to come inside. Locking the door again behind them, she led them to a surprisingly cozy sitting room.

Too excited to sit down, Winter paced. "My mother. Where is she?"

"I don't know. The man who took you came back, and she left with him. I told her not to trust him, but she was desperate to find you." She shook her head. "Let me start at the beginning. It will make more sense."

Trace crossed to Winter, gently pulling her over to sit beside him on an aging sofa. The arm he placed around her shoulder was so much more comforting than anything else she could imagine. "Sit. Listen. This is why you came."

The old woman perched on the edge of a worn leather chair. Steepling her hands in front of her, she began to talk. "Kathleen came here almost twenty-three years ago. She was young, and full of life. She'd landed a job at the offices of the Alliance, and she was dating a dashing young officer there. She thought her life was perfect. She'd sit right where you are now, and tell me about how they were going to get married and buy a house and live happily ever after."

"And did they? Get married?" It occurred to her that they hadn't lived happily ever after.

The woman shook her head sadly. "No. Her young man got her with child, but he said he couldn't marry her yet because it would screw up his chances of a big promotion that he'd been angling for. He took care of her though, and made sure she had everything she needed. The pregnancy went well, and eventually she delivered a lovely little girl child. That would be you. She was so happy, and the officer looked like he would be a great dad. He spent a lot of time with you, and celebrated every one of your young accomplishments. Then, when you were about three, he took you away. He said he was taking you for ice cream and he never came back. Your mother went crazy trying to find you. At first she thought the pair of you had been in an accident but days went by and she couldn't find you. She finally managed to get into the barracks, and the sergeant in charge told her the truth. The man she loved had chosen her as a brood mare for his child. He was assigned to an experimental facility, and he'd wanted a child with his DNA to be part of the trials. So, he'd seduced your mother, gotten her pregnant and when you were old enough he'd taken you to the lab."

Winter let out a shocked squeak. "No! My father planned to send me to that lab before I was even born?"

Greta nodded. "I'm afraid so. Your mother spent almost two years trying to find you without success. The thought of you alone and scared in some laboratory almost drove her insane. Then one evening, the asshole came back. He said he'd take her to you, if she agreed to go right then. I told her not to, told her he couldn't be trusted but she said she had to. She loved you, and if there were any chance of her seeing you again, she had to take it. She left with him, and I never saw her again."

Winter felt like someone had punched her in the gut. She'd found out that her mother had loved her and wanted her. That felt good, but she'd also found out that her father had turned her over to that hellhole, and he'd been fully aware of what went on there. That meant he was one of the monsters, and she'd probably been in contact with him. The thought made her sick.

"Can you tell us a bit about her mother, about Kathleen?" Trace rubbed a hand down her arm. "It would mean a lot if to us."

The old lady jumped to her feet. "I can do better than that. I have some of her things. When she didn't come back, I put them in a box in the hall closet. I'll get it for you." She hurried out of the room.

"Thank you." Winter forced the words out. "For asking about my mother."

"No sweat. Concentrate on her. She loved you."

"But my father sold me out, probably before I was born."

"Then he'd better hope I never meet him."

She almost smiled then. Almost. Trust Trace to boil it all down to such a simple statement. He'd never do something like that to his own child.

"Here you go." Greta hurried back into the room with a cardboard box. "There's some pictures in here, and some other things."

Winter sat the box in her lap and gingerly opened the lid.

* * *

It had been over an hour since they'd left the boarding house, but she still felt like she were in a dream, like she'd wake up any minute and find out it had all been a nightmare. Trace had pulled the jeep over in a deserted back lane so he could wrap her up in his big arms.

"Want to talk about it?"

She shook her head.

"Okay then. Let me know when you're ready to get moving again. We've got lots of time."

Winter gave a barely perceptible nod of her head. She should really tell him what this was all about, why she'd developed this sudden obsession with her past but this wasn't the right time. Not yet. Not while she was still reeling from the revelations of the past few hours.

"I'm going to have a child." Why had she blurted that out? She held her breath, waiting for Trace's reaction. It seemed to take forever before he finally spoke.

"You're pregnant now, or you're planning on it?"

"Now. I'm pregnant now."

"Well, shit." Silence reigned for an endless moment. He kept his arms around her, and she hoped that was a good sign. "I'm the father?" Wonder filled his voice.

She nodded against his shoulder, afraid that her voice would fail her.

"That night in the gravel pit. You conceived that night? We took precautions."

"Precautions don't work so well on me. One of the improvements the lab doctors concocted. They wanted to use me as a brood mare."

"That's disgusting."

Winter whimpered, unable to hide her distress. This was so humiliating.

"I didn't mean you. You're amazing. The doctors and the whole lab thing, that's what's disgusting."

"Are you mad? I'm not going to try to trap you or anything. I just thought you should know."

Trace moved his hand lower, until its warmth lay directly over her womb. "I've never even considered being a father. It'll take some getting used to, but you must know I care about you and I promise I will protect you and our child to the best of my ability. Love at first sight is such a corny theory, but from the first moment I kissed you in that gravel pit, I knew we were meant to be together. I was going to take it slow, court you like a normal guy, but this kind of speeds things up, don't you think?"

Winter lifted her face, staring up into his dark eyes. Why had she ever thought they were glacial?

Trace placed his hand under her chin, tilting it up so he could ravage her lips in the gentlest of kisses. "Girl or boy?"

Winter ran the tip of her tongue across her lips, savoring the taste of him. "Yes, it will be one or the other. I haven't gone to see a doctor, haven't seen one since I escaped from the lab. I'm afraid they'd see something and realize who I am. What I am. Much too risky."

"That could be an issue. If you're going to have a child you need to see a doctor."

Winter shook her head. "I don't think so. One of my sisters is a midwife. She can take care of whatever I need."

Trace narrowed his eyes. "If I can find a real doctor who's not connected to the government, will you agree to see him? Or her?"

Winter sighed. "Is *maybe* a good enough answer? It would depend on how safe I think it is."

Trace grinned. "I can work with a maybe." He enveloped her in the biggest bear hug she'd ever experienced. "I'm going to be a daddy!"

"And you'll be a great one!"

For the first time in a long time, she felt at peace. Between her and Trace and their extended families, they would make sure that this child, this tiny being born out of their love would be cherished and protected at all times.

The future spread out in front of them with infinite possibilities, all of them full of hope and love.

Snake Eyes (Mercenaries 5)

Anne Kane

Snake may not be the nicest guy you ever met, but he has his own code of honor, and he does everything in his power to live up to it. Keeping his hands off his Sergeant's sister-in-law, no matter how sexy she is, is definitely in the code.

Wren has the hots for Snake but she's frustrated that he can't seem to see her as anything other than Dee's kid sister. When she sees him sneak out after dark, she suspects he's going to meet a lover and follows him, determined to finally make him see her as the mature sexy woman she is. Unfortunately, things don't go exactly according to plan. She manages to get herself captured and Snake is forced to come to her rescue.

Chapter One

Snake stalked slowly toward her, a lethal mix of grace and feral strength. The light of the full moon played across his face, highlighting the scars from hundreds of fights. His cheeks were angular, the chin solid and unyielding. Mothers warned their daughters about men like Snake, men whose eyes were haunted with the memories of things best left unsaid.

And yet, what captured Wren's attention was his mouth. Warm. Sensual. Sinfully tempting. She got goose bumps just looking at his mouth. The imagined feel of those lips on her skin sent her libido soaring.

A shiver of sheer longing went through her as he reached her and wrapped his brawny arms around her. Snake lowered his mouth and a low groan escaped her lips, a mixture of satisfaction and anticipation. Their breath mingling, he ran his tongue the length of her lips, demanding entrance. She complied without hesitation, melting against his hard body.

He had endless patience. Taking his time, he held her close as he explored the inside of her mouth. Starting off gently, as if he were afraid to spook her, his touch quickly became bolder, more urgent. His tongue delved aggressively, investigating every inch, taking possession wherever it touched.

The feel of his body pressed tight against hers sent shivers of desire careening up Wren's spine. The hard length of his cock pressed into her belly, teasing her, inviting her to imagine all sorts of sinfully naughty things. She wriggled suggestively, loving how it felt to grind herself against the tangible evidence of his desire.

She'd wanted him for so long, waited impatiently for him to see her as more than just the kid sister of his buddy's woman. Finally, just when she thought it would never happen, here he was, his hands busily tugging at the stays holding her shirt closed. It didn't take long for him to figure out the string fastenings and bare her breasts to his gaze.

She hadn't bothered with a bra this morning, reveling in the feeling of freedom that came with the loose fitted top. Her breasts stood at attention under his hungry gaze, the tips puckering at the measured flick of his tongue. Darts of liquid fire danced down her spine as he settled in to worship the sensitive mounds with his mouth, the gentle scrape of his teeth across her flesh causing her to whimper with need.

God, that felt so good!

Wren reveled in the sensations washing through her, loving the way her body responded to Snake's touch. Soon though, the need for more overwhelmed her. She pushed him away and quickly divested herself of the rest of her clothing, tossing the garments carelessly to the ground.

Snake took advantage of the brief respite to shed his own clothes before reaching out to pull her back into his arms. Heat kindled in those dark eyes of his as he wrapped his arms around her, urging her closer. She didn't resist. She could feel the hard length of him pressing against her as she arched into his embrace. Thrusting her tongue into his mouth, she twined it around his, tempting him to do more, to give in to the demon of lust that rode them both. He opened his eyes, staring down at her and she saw the raw desire burning there.

He laid her down on the soft grass, stretching himself out beside her. As he smoothed his hand over her belly, Wren felt a familiar molten heat ignite deep inside her. Only this time, it would be different. It wasn't going to end in frustration. Snake was here with her, touching her, preparing to make love to her.

Finally!

Her breath caught in her throat as the big mercenary trailed his hand across the exposed skin of her mound, bared to the cool night air. Darts of erotic flame danced deep inside her, anticipation making each touch of his fingers all the more intense.

She'd waited so long for him to notice her, to make a move, to take her up on the endless parade of silent invitations she'd thrown his way over the last few months. She was a grown woman and she knew what she wanted, but Snake had taken what felt like an eternity to come to the same conclusion. She let out a low moan as his fingers explored the soft folds guarding her entrance.

She wanted Snake to be hers, and she intended to have him. Tonight was the first time she'd managed to get past his stoic you're-off-limits attitude and she didn't plan to waste the opportunity. Dampness gathered at the apex of her thighs as he continued to stroke his fingers through the delicate folds of skin.

She sucked in a deep breath as his thumb grazed across the hard nub of her clit. Naked lust flared with every touch of his hand, every slide of his tongue along hers. She couldn't get enough of him. Running her hand down the smooth length of his cock, she marveled at the sheer size. This was what she did to him, how his body reacted to her presence, her touch. The heady intoxication of her power over this rough, tough mercenary flooded her.

She circled his shaft with one hand, slowly tracing the length of it. Long and thick, it pulsed under her eager fingers. Snake twined his fingers in her long hair, a guttural sound escaping his throat as he urged her toward him.

Mesmerized by the sight of his shaft bobbing gently in front of her, Wren flicked her tongue out to taste the single drop of pre cum glistening on the flared head. He tasted salty, and undeniably male.

She scored her tongue along the slit in the tip and was rewarded by a strangled oath from above. He said something, but she couldn't quite make out the words.

It didn't matter. She knew what he wanted.

Sliding her mouth over the thick head, she sucked his massive cock in and swirled her tongue around the shaft. Tasting. Teasing. The sensation of having him helplessly in her power added a heady edge of excitement. After all this time, she finally had him right where she wanted him.

Naked and hard.

Every move of her tongue, every nibble of her teeth brought a reaction. She bobbed her head back and forth, sliding it over the rigid shaft. Slowly, she increased the speed, experimenting with the pressure of her lips until he let out a frustrated oath.

"No!" The sound exploded from him in a single breath. "I want to be inside you when I come."

He pulled himself out of her mouth, and Wren raised her head to look into his eyes. The stark expression on his face rocked her. She wondered at the strength of character it took to stop at just that point.

Then he scooped her up in his arms, his mouth coming down to devour hers, and all rational thought vanished. Again. He tended to have that effect on her.

Laying her gently on the ground, he traced her curves with reverent fingers. "I spend every night dreaming of you, of what I would do to you if you were mine."

He paused, running a hand over the curve of her hip. Barely above a whisper, his voice betrayed the depths of his feelings. "I never thought I stood a chance with you. You're special. You deserve so much more than I can offer you."

Without waiting for a reaction, he lowered his head to taste the smooth skin of her belly, the tip of his tongue following his hand over her hips. He covered her breast with the other hand, shaping the sensitive flesh with his fingers.

Wren closed her eyes and let the sensations wash over her. Lust curled through her body, and she couldn't hold still beneath his marauding hands. "I need you."

"I know." He nipped the skin on her inner thigh, his breath hot on her skin. "Open up for me." She spread her legs, allowing him access to the soft folds guarding the entrance to her sex. Not even the tiniest scrap of lace barred his way.

A tiny moan escaped her lips as he used his tongue to find the little bundle of nerves at her clit. The sensation, so intense it bordered on painful, left her gasping for breath and she clung to him as heat flared through every nerve.

"So good, so very good." He whispered the words against her, as he tasted her most private parts, his tongue delving deep to plunder the nectar at her very center.

Wren arched into his mouth as he thrust his tongue repeatedly into her damp heat. He slid one finger inside her, pumping it in and out, increasing the pace as her body responded to a rhythm as old as time itself.

"You're driving me insane." She barely managed to gasp the words out.

"Glad to hear it." He lowered his face to rake his teeth across her clit, and she lost the ability to speak. She felt the orgasm begin at her toes, sweeping up through her and pushing everything but the wave of incredible pleasure out of its way. Her lips parted just as Snake surged up over her, taking the strangled scream from her lips as her orgasm peaked.

He braced himself on one elbow and slid a condom over his shaft before guiding his hard cock to her pussy lips. She let out a second cry, one of welcome as he plunged deep inside.

She felt incredibly full; overwhelmed by the sheer naked lust that refused to let her out of its clutches.

Snake cupped her face with one hand, and she let her eyelids flutter open. His eyes were deep pools of desire, burning hot in his face. She could see the incredible effort it took him to stop, to give her time to adjust to his possession of her. He was so damn big, much bigger than any other man she'd ever known.

In response to his wordless question, she wrapped her arms around his neck and pulled him down on top of her.

He began to move. Slowly at first, thrusting balls deep before withdrawing almost completely. Long powerful thrusts of his hips sent the fires burning once more through the depths of her body.

Wren closed her eyes and gave herself up to the sheer pleasure of the moment. Wrapping her legs around Snake's muscular waist, she locked her heels behind his back and matched him thrust for thrust.

Within minutes she could feel the momentum building once again, pushing her toward a release that glittered, tantalizing, just beyond her reach. Darts of liquid heat pranced across every inch of naked skin.

Snake thrust hard one last time, clutching her close and letting out a primal yell of triumph as his hot seed spurted out.

The sound triggered Wren's own release, flinging her off the edge of sanity and into the vast universe beyond. She caught her breath as a thousand tiny aftershocks rocked through her, leaving her panting and shell-shocked with sheer pleasure.

As the waves of pleasure slowly subsided, Snake rolled off to his side without letting her go. They lay there, locked together, and for just a brief moment Wren got an inkling of what it would be like to be Snake's woman, to know that these strong arms would always be there to hold and protect her.

She kept her eyes firmly closed for the longest time, avoiding the inevitable return to reality.

Chapter Two

Two weeks later...

Wren watched from deep in the shadows of the doorway as Snake slung a leg over his motorcycle and fired it up. *Where the hell is he going?*

She'd finally worked up the courage to confront him about their relationship, or lack thereof and he was buggering off into the night? Without any of the other guys on the team? *Well, shit.*

She felt a heavy lump of dread forming in the pit of her stomach. He was going out at night. Alone. Without his buddies. Not a lot of reasons for doing that came to mind.

Except a woman.

As in another woman. A woman who wasn't her. Was that why he'd been ignoring her? She'd thought they were finally making progress, but maybe that wonderful night they'd spent together had been a huge mistake on his part. Hell, maybe he'd had another woman all along.

Snake pulled on his helmet and dropped the bike into gear, roaring out of the compound without as much as a backward glance.

Then again, it's not like he knew she was lurking in the shadows spying on him.

She took a deep, steadying breath. Only one thing to do, really. She needed some answers.

Hurrying back inside, she grabbed the keys to the jeep.

* * *

He wasn't all that hard to follow. At this time of night, the roads were almost deserted, and Snake's motorcycle was loud. Very loud. The hardest part of the whole thing was making sure Snake didn't realize someone was stalking him.

Despite the lump of lead in her stomach, she felt the corner of her mouth curve upward at the thought of her being a stalker. Amazing how life could change. Less than a year ago she'd had a heavy collar around her neck, and lived in a locked cage. Now she was stalking a guy she'd made wild love to in a moonlit clearing, and she thought he might be seeing someone else. Funny how things worked out in life. If there were a deity in charge of all this, she had one hell of a sense of humor!

In this area of town the houses were mostly brick, set on large lots with real trees and grass surrounding them. Definitely the rich side of town.

She rounded a corner and found herself almost on top of Snake and his bike. He'd pulled off to the side of the road and was busy securing his helmet to the lock behind the seat.

Struggling to recover her equilibrium Wren kept going, praying he was too focused on his own agenda to recognize the jeep. Circling the block, she managed to find a parking space farther up the street where she could watch him from a distance. Unfortunately by the time she managed that, all she saw was the tail end of his boot going over a rock wall.

Odd. She couldn't see Snake as the kind of guy to have a thing with someone else's woman, but why else would he park his bike and jump a wall into the back of someone's property? She felt the knot in her stomach relax a tiny bit. Maybe he wasn't involved with another woman. There had to be something else going on here. But what?

Only one way to find out. Checking to make sure her com-unit was firmly fastened around her wrist, she smoothed her hair back and hopped out onto the sidewalk.

She took her time, strolling along as if she didn't have a care in the world. She passed the spot where Snake's feet had disappeared, but kept going. Even if she thought she could vault over such a high wall, it didn't seem like the best of ideas. She had no idea what was waiting for her on the other side.

She kept walking until she came to a massive set of wrought iron gates that blocked entry to some type of huge estate. A long driveway led from the locked gates to a cluster of buildings in the distance. There seemed to be a lot of people scurrying to and fro but that was one damn long driveway, and the people were too far away for Wren to see what they were doing. It looked more like a military facility than a home, and Wren's curiosity kicked into high gear. Where the heck did Snake fit into this picture?

Since he hadn't entered by the main gate, or any gate at all for that matter, she had to assume he didn't want to be seen. *Maybe this is some kind of espionage mission?* Grasping the cold iron gates with both hands, she strained to see what the people at the far end of the driveway were doing.

Within seconds, two guards materialized out of the decorative gatehouse, startling her into taking a step back. She hadn't realized the gatehouse was manned. The younger of the two smiled at her, but the warmth didn't extend to his eyes. His hand went to the butt of the holstered gun at his waist, caressing it in a rather disturbing fashion. "Can we help you?"

She shook her head, survival instincts kicking into high gear now. These guys did not want to help her. She'd bet her last cred chip on it. "No. I was just out for a walk and stopped to admire the lovely stone wall." She gestured at the towering six-foot high rock wall on either side of the gates. "It's very beautiful. Who lives here?"

The guard shook his head, a slight frown furrowing his brow. "Sorry, I can't quite hear you."

He motioned her closer, and idiot that she was, she took that fatal step forward.

She didn't see it coming. The taser took her down instantly and the two guards rushed out to grab her, dragging her through the narrow walking gate and into the guard hut. With chilling efficiency they removed her com-unit and secured her arms behind her back with a cable tie, then gagged her so that she couldn't scream for help.

As if that were an option. The simple art of breathing was taking all her concentration right now. That taser packed one hell of a punch. She lay on the cold tile floor, unable to regain control of her limbs. One guard kept a close watch on her, while the older of the two called for instructions.

She groaned inwardly. What had she managed to get herself mixed up in this time?

By the time they grabbed her on either side and began to frog-march her across the open compound square toward a two-story building, she had mostly recovered from the effects of the taser, but she was still no match for two well-armed guards. No matter how much she twisted and squirmed she couldn't free herself from the pair.

What did Snake have to do with this place? The other woman theory had bit the dust about the same time she did.

They marched her up a set of imposing stone stairs and into the building, ignoring the fact that her calves and feet were bruised and raw in places from the rough treatment. She'd lost one of her shoes when they dragged her through the gate, and most of her hair had escaped from its ponytail. She suspected she looked more look like a refugee from the Alliance holding tanks than a lovesick idiot trying to find out where her lover spent his nights. How did she manage to get herself into these messes?

The doors opened into a large hall, and the two guards wasted no time in dragging her across the hall. Although there were several other people in the building, no one seemed to think it odd that a woman with a gag in her mouth was being dragged, against her will, through the entrance. The guards herded her into a smaller side room and thrust her into a metal cage in the center.

Okay, this was definitely some kind of military facility. The smirk on the younger guard's face as the two turned to leave left her with a nasty taste in her mouth. Where the hell was Snake and what was he up to? This didn't make any sense at all, and while she highly doubted he had a lady friend stashed somewhere in this hellhole, it seemed equally unlikely that he was somehow mixed up with these guys.

She gave her head a mental shake. Maybe she needed to rethink her modus operandi. After being kidnapped and held in a fighting arena last year, you'd think she'd be smart enough to avoid this kind of thing, but no. Here she was again. Jumping in with both feet before finding out what was going on didn't seem to be working so well for her.

She looked around the room carefully, making sure there weren't any other nasty guys lurking in the corners before she tested her bonds. Sadly, she had more than a little bit of experience in trying to escape from bondage. Flexing her hands, she found enough slack in the ties to slip her hands free. Well at least something was going in her favor!

For now, though, she slipped her hands back into the restraints. She was in a cage, and given the military flavor of this place it was highly possible she was being watched on a vid feed. She'd save that surprise for when it might actually help her to escape. The last thing she wanted right now was for the smiling young guard to return and do a better job of securing her.

* * *

From his hiding place behind a particularly fragrant flowering bush, Snake watched two burly guards drag a woman toward the main building. She wasn't going willingly, twisting and squirming wildly between them. The scene definitely lent credence to the rumors he'd heard about this place. His gut reaction was to leap over the bush, beat the shit out of the two goons, and rescue the damsel in distress. Unfortunately, that wasn't currently an option.

He clenched his fist, but forced himself to remain still. The purpose of this trip was intelligence, finding out what was going on. Interfering with anything at this point would blow that right out of the water.

He'd overheard a conversation at one of the local pubs that implied the lost children project had been resurrected again. If he saw anything that bore that premise out, he'd take it back to the rest of the guys and together they'd decide what to do about it. Several of their girlfriends had been involved in that horrific experiment, and the thought of it being restarted wouldn't go over well with women or the rest of the group of mercenaries.

The woman tossed her head, her long blonde hair swinging sideways in a sleek cascade and for a brief moment he got a clear look at her face, including her terrified blue eyes. An invisible fist slammed him right in the gut.

Wren!

What the hell was she doing here? After being abducted by a fighting ring and then rescued by Snake and his buddies less than a year ago, Wren would surely be smart enough to stay well away from guys who viewed females as little more than animals to be used and discarded. Apparently not. His little bird seemed to have a knack for getting herself into trouble.

Suddenly, tonight's outing became upgraded from eyes-only to a rescue mission. There was no way in hell he was leaving here without the feisty beauty who'd stolen his heart the first moment he'd seen her. He might not be good enough for her, but he was way better than the scum who ran this place.

It had been over a decade since rumors of the lost children had been bandied about. It was said that the government had conducted experiments on street orphans, turning the unfortunate waifs into human/computer hybrids who could infiltrate a computer network or electronic installation at the touch of a hand. The cybernetic beings they created were incredibly talented; able to connect themselves to all types of electronic equipment with a mere touch and bypass the harshest security protocols to obtain classified information. The government had been ecstatic at first, picturing a whole new step in man's evolution and their own control over the population.

Their elation had been short-lived. The children had proved too volatile to control.

He looked around, narrowing his eyes as he assessed the sparse cover available in the compound. Out here, there was not much chance of making a move to snatch Wren back. Low, barrack style buildings lined both sides of an open central square. To the left a high stone wall bordered the heavy iron gates, which appeared to have at least two guards in attendance at all times. To his right sat a massive two-story block building. He eyed it thoughtfully. Given the amount of traffic coming and going through the colossal front doors, it had to house the main offices and administration areas.

His felt his heart twist helplessly in his chest as Wren disappeared through those doors, but throwing himself on two heavily-armed soldiers would be pure suicide. He hadn't felt so helpless since he'd seen his entire family gunned down by the rebels during the provincial wars.

How the hell had Wren ended up being dragged through this compound by two goons? He'd deliberately avoided telling anyone about this place until he was sure of his facts so calling in backup would take time, and time was the one thing he didn't have much of if he wanted to get Wren out of here before anything nasty happened.

He needed to get himself a plan. He liked plans. Plans meant he had control of the situation and he was all about control.

Rising silently to his feet, he glided along the length of the hedge, hesitating to confirm no one was looking before he drifted across the open grass toward the main building. The key to not being noticed was to look like you belonged, and in a compound full of beefy soldier types, he could blend in without any problem at all.

He managed to cross the full width of the compound without anyone challenging him. Reaching his target building, he didn't hesitate. Taking the stairs at a quick clip, he made it to the wide landing at the top and pulled open the towering front doors. No one batted an eye as he entered the massive main hall.

Now all he had to do was find his girl.

* * *

Wren's heartbeat jumped as the door opened and the younger of the two guards re-entered the room, followed by a tough-looking guy in military fatigues. The latter strode up to the cage, circling her with a thoughtful look on his face. He reminded her of the trainers at the fight facility she'd been held hostage in, and the thought did nothing to make her feel better about her current situation. Instinctively, she turned in the small cage so that she faced him at all times.

Don't ever let them see you flinch. Amazing how quickly the survival tips she'd learned at that facility came back to her.

"Interesting." The man folded his hands behind his back, his cold gaze moving slowly from the tips of her feet upward until he was staring her straight in the eyes. "You say she just showed up at the gate?"

The young guard nodded. "Yes sir, Major. Said she was admiring the grounds or something. She didn't even try to get away. Obviously had no clue."

Something about the man's eyes reminded Wren of a reptile. Cold. Emotionless. Raising her chin, she held the man's gaze until he looked away, a mirthless smile on his face. Given her current predicament she didn't really feel good about anything at the moment, but she had a particularly bad feeling about this guy.

"Good call, Baxter. We could use some new bloodlines to strengthen the stock. We'll have her vetted by the Doc, and run her through basics of course, but if everything checks out she'll make a nice addition to our stable. I'll make sure you get a commendation for your initiative in procuring her."

"Sir. Thank you, sir." The guard saluted crisply, a grin curving the corner of his mouth as the other man moved over to the desk and began to fill out some forms. After a moment's hesitation he cleared his throat loudly.

The older man looked up. "Is there something else?"

The guard nodded. "Yes, sir."

Silence reigned for a moment. "Well?"

The guard shuffled his feet, looking suddenly nervous. "I haven't been assigned a female of my own yet and I know I scored well on the aptitude tests. I just thought… well… since I found her…" His voice trailed off, but Wren had the sickening suspicion she knew exactly what he was asking for.

The older man glanced over at her speculatively, and Wren had to fight not to shrink into a corner of the cage and hide from his too-knowing gaze. What the hell had she gotten herself into?

"Find the little bitch attractive, do you, son?"

The guard mumbled a reply.

The major nodded. "You're a good lad, and you're right. You captured her so you deserve first crack at her. I'll put a good word in for you with the Doc. If everything checks out, you just might have your own bitch to train."

"Thank you, Major, sir! You won't be disappointed." The guard saluted again, turning to devour her with his gaze before marching smartly to the door and departing.

Probably going to see if there were any other innocent women wandering the streets that he could kidnap.

The major signed the bottom of the paper with a flourish and put the pen down. Straightening up, he strolled back over to the cage. He looked like career military rather than mercenary, although Wren doubted that this facility was on any of the government's official plans. His hair was cut short, his uniform wrinkle free and his boots polished to a high shine. He produced an instant camera and pointed it at her. The flash damn near blinded her, and by the time her vision cleared the man was clipping a small photo of her to the corner of the papers he'd been writing on.

Something about the uniform teased the edge of her memory although she couldn't quite place her finger on it. Palace guard? Alliance Special Forces? Maybe some kind of elite offshoot of the regular troops? Those stripes did indicate a major's rank, not that his rank made any difference to her. As soon as he left the room she intended to get out of this cage and make a break for it. Snake had one hell of a lot of explaining to do when she got back home.

She jumped at the sound of his voice. "Ready for your physical? The Doc will be happy to see a new recruit. Been awhile since we added a bitch to the program."

The most terrifying thing about that question was the total lack of innuendo in the major's voice. He might as well have been discussing the weather, or what was for supper. Still, she had no intention of giving in to whatever new type of hell she'd put herself in line for. Maybe a little bravado was called for.

"I want out. Now. Those men had no reason to grab me. I'm a citizen and I demand you release me."

Something that vaguely resembled mirth appeared in the major's eyes. "Feisty little thing. I like that. I'll enjoy following your training, but first we need to get you into the system." Raising his wrist to his face, he keyed a wrist-mounted com-unit and barked out a series of commands in a language she couldn't quite follow. Russian maybe? Or Chinese? Who the hell were these guys?

The reply was just as indecipherable, but it obviously wasn't what he'd wanted to hear. Turning on his heels he stomped out of the room without another word.

Good.

Slipping her wrists free, Wren squatted down to inspect the lock on her cage. Lucky for her, lock picking had been a required skill when she and her sister had been living on the streets. She just hoped this one was susceptible to the assortment of pins she used to adorn her hair. With any luck she'd be out of here in minutes!

She froze at the sound of footsteps echoing in the corridor outside. Cursing softly, she hurried to replace the pins and slip her wrists back into the cable tie before she backed away to the far side of the cage.

She felt like a cornered rat, watching the door in dread as the footsteps came closer.

Chapter Three

The door burst open with a high-pitched squeal of hinges. The major was back, along with yet another couple of burly guards wheeling a medical gurney between them. There seemed to be an endless supply of muscular young men in this place, and unfortunately none of them were on her side.

One of the new arrivals strode up to the cage, and as she turned to keep her attention on the new threat, she felt a pinprick in her butt.

Her eyes widened at the knowing look on the face of the man facing her. Seriously? Tranquilizer darts? Did they have an aversion to handling a conscious woman? If she ever managed to get herself free, she'd give them a reason for that aversion. Her vision started to blur. *Great. Here we go again.*

"Damn." By the time the word left her mouth she was already sinking to the floor, the tranquilizer in the dart flooding through her body with ruthless efficiency.

The man facing her unlocked the cage door and the two of them lifted her limp form onto the gurney. She wasn't sure what was worse, the fact that she was still conscious enough to know what was going on or the fact that she was powerless to stop it.

They rolled her on her side and snipped the cable ties holding her hands so that they could lay her on the gurney more efficiently, fastening her hands to the sides of the cold metal tray. She could only hope they were as sloppy with restraints as the first guard had been.

The taller of the two spoke over top of her, as if she weren't there. Or worse, as if she didn't matter.

"The Doc said he's got an opening now so he'll examine her shortly."

"Good." The major nodded. "I'll come watch. I promised Baxter I'd put in a good word for him when the time came to assign a trainer for her."

The other medic grinned. "Baxter's been itching to get a bitch for a while now. He'd do a good job on her, maybe even get her qualified for mission duty."

The first medic guffawed, and the sound sent a chill down Wren's paralyzed spine. "I'm betting she'll be breeding long before that happens. You know the Doc wants some young ones to work with, and this one looks prime for the breeding program."

"True." The major casually reached over and ran a too-familiar hand down her hips. "She's young and strong, good wide hips. Probably be able to drop a youngster and be back in the field the next day. Just what we need for this program -- females who can breed and fight at the same time. Get her up to medical, and tell the Doc to go ahead with an exam. I'm late for the evening rotation with my squadron, or I'd talk to him myself. Tell him I'll contact him later to discuss the results."

"Yes, sir." The medic grasped the lead edge of the gurney and maneuvered it out the door. "The Doc will want to do a thorough work-up on her if she's going into the breeding program. We can get the blood work out of the way while we're waiting for him."

* * *

Snake slid around the corner of the hallway, listening intently. The conversation between the two men in the room sent a chill right through him. He'd love to think that it wasn't Wren they were discussing but he wasn't that naïve. He still wasn't sure what the place was, but he knew he didn't want her here, now or ever.

He'd been captivated by the tiny beauty ever since they'd rescued her from the fighting rings in Loden province. Being the younger sister of Sergeant's gal though, meant she was off limits to a guy like him. She was sweet and naïve and deserved better, but that didn't stop his cock from being in a semi-permanent state of arousal ever since he'd set eyes on her. She was everything he wanted and could never have. Young, sweet, with dusky skin and long blonde hair, she made him wish he were a better man, the kind of man who got married and had kids. The kind of man who raised a family and went on Sunday picnics in the park.

Hell, he'd never been that kind of guy. Raised on the wrong side of the gyro on the outer rim of Jupiter, he'd always known he was what the gentler folk called space trash. With no father and a mother who spent most of her time in a drug-induced fog that she paid for with her body, he'd practically raised himself. He'd learned early on how to make himself as invisible as he could in order to steal enough food to stave off the ever present hunger pangs.

When he was around twelve, he'd tried to lift a raft of meat from the locker of a merchant vessel inbound for Earth. Lucky for him, that vessel belonged to Kaeden. The Sarge had a soft spot for misfits and he'd given him a choice. Get sent to juvenile lock up, or join the ship's crew as cabin boy and work off his debt.

He'd been part of the group ever since, having earned their respect in countless ways over the last decade and a half. He'd never forgotten that he owed his life to the Sarge though, and there was no way he'd repay him by taking advantage of Kaeden's little sister-in-law.

No way. Not even if this huge, rock solid, ever present hard-on killed him.

The sound of a door opening signaled the end of the conversation. Apparently the door in front of him wasn't the only way in and out of that room. He waited a few precious seconds, hearing nothing but a resounding silence. Moving slowly, he turned the doorknob and slid into the room. An empty metal cage dominated the center of the room. The door to the cage stood open but he knew deep down in his gut that Wren had been in that cage until moments ago. *Damn*!

Assessing the sparse furniture in the room, he crossed to the battered oak desk in the corner. The form on top caught his immediate attention. A picture of Wren in the cage was paper-clipped to the upper corner and a rather crass description of her physical attributes filled the page. Yup, she was here all right, but why? He had the sickening feeling that this was somehow his fault, but even if it wasn't, it was up to him to get her out. And fast. He still had no proof of what this facility was but he was sure it wasn't good news.

He crossed to the door on the far side of the room, silently peering out. It opened onto what appeared to be a large reception area, with men busily crisscrossing it from all directions. Some of them had females with them, although it was obvious that the men were in charge. The women all stayed a step behind the men, their focus completely on the man in front of them. At least half of the women were at some stage of pregnancy, which seemed incredibly odd for a military facility.

The conversation he'd overheard had mentioned taking her to a medical facility, so he needed to find that. His ability to blend in without being noticed was going to be tested to its limits today. Taking a deep breath, he strode out into the large hall.

Keep walking. Look like you belong. Don't slow down long enough to be noticed. All the old adages came back easily as he unobtrusively scanned the many doors leading out of the hall. Sticking close to the edges of the hall he submerged himself in the flow of people. They all seemed to be on their way to somewhere important, totally ignoring the stranger in their midst. Then again, maybe they were used to strangers coming and going.

He hit pay dirt on the north side of the hall when a young cadet opened a door to what appeared to be the infirmary. He caught a glimpse of a hospital type room, with a large metal table in the middle, and sprawled across that table was Wren.

Increasing his pace, he managed to slip through the door before it closed and ghosted himself behind a curtain used to cordon off an exam cubicle. He could hear several men talking on the far side of the room, and when he peered out he could see them bent over a desk littered with paperwork.

"We don't know where she came from, or why. We should just terminate her and dispose of the remains."

"Not so fast." An older man, with a mop of grey hair and a commanding voice picked up a metal clipboard. "She appears to be young and healthy, and we need more breeding bitches to bring us up to the desired quota. If her physical and blood work are good, I think we should put her into training and see how she works out. No point in wasting a perfectly good specimen. It's not like we can just let her go at this point."

"And if someone comes looking for her?"

He shrugged. "We can deal with that if it happens, and why would they come looking here? We're a training facility for off-world medics. We're not open to the public."

The younger man shook his head, looking far from convinced. "Personally, I think it's too risky, but let's do the physical and blood work. We already have a soldier willing to take her on as a trainee." He picked up another clipboard and flipped over the pages. "Private Baxter. I remember the lad, young but enthusiastic. The major speaks very highly of him. He scored excellent on the last round of tests, just the right combination of loyalty to the cause, and good solid genetics. He'll make an excellent sperm donor, and be proud as punch to have offspring in the enhancement program."

Snake definitely didn't like the sound of that. Sperm donor? He needed to get Wren out of here ASAP. Moving silently, he brushed the side of the curtain, moving it enough that he could see into the main room.

Wren lay motionless on the metal table. Her arms and legs sprawled at awkward angles as if they'd tossed her there without a care as to her comfort. Snake clenched his teeth, making a physical effort not to barge in and wring the two men's necks. Somehow it seemed a million times worse when the woman being mistreated was his.

He gave his head a mental shake. She wasn't his. She could never be his, but that didn't mean he wouldn't protect her to his dying breath.

The older of the two men handed the clipboard to the other and moved to stand beside the table, talking all the while. The bastard must have a mic on him, recording the session.

"Subject appears to be in her twenties. Good bone structure. No obvious flaws. Muscle development on arms and legs indicate a healthy regime. I surmise a high probability of her being able to withstand training." He ran his hands impersonally over her body, and Snake once again had to restrain himself. Only the impersonal nature of the inspection saved the damned doctor from immediately becoming intimately acquainted with whatever deity he believed in.

"No evidence of exposure to radiation or any prior injuries that might jeopardize the intended use of the specimen. We will now take blood and tissues and have them analyzed to confirm health and fertility."

The second doctor handed him a syringe and several small vials. After extracting half a dozen vials of blood, the doctor pulled a thin cotton sheet over the unconscious woman. Handing over the clipboard, he addressed his colleague. "That's it for now. Take her down to a holding room until she recovers consciousness. The test results should be back in a couple of hours, and depending on the results we can make a final recommendation."

"Don't you want to do an internal exam as well?" The younger doctor's brow furrowed.

Snake held his breath. If that asshole dared to do something as intimate as an internal exam while Wren lay there unable to defend herself, he wasn't sure he'd be able to contain himself.

Wisely, the doctor shook his head. "No need at this point, and I'm already late for my staff meeting. I'll be back to check on the results of the blood test before mess call tonight. If everything checks out, we can do an internal at that point."

The younger man nodded. "Very well, sir."

Snake let the curtain drop and held his breath as the doctor strode out of the room. He could hear the other man fiddling in the main part of the room, opening and closing drawers. The sound of a door closing preceded an eerie quiet.

What the hell? He should be able to see anyone exiting the room.

Carefully lifting the corner of the curtain he looked into the main room. Empty. Wren was gone. He took two strides into the room before he saw the door on the far wall. A second exit! Shit! He'd thought that was a closet.

Now he needed to find her all over again!

Schooling his features into an expressionless glare that he'd found made most people hesitate to approach, much less question him, he yanked the second door open and strode through.

A long corridor stretched out in front of him, broken up every ten feet or so by a closed door. Must be the administrative section. Hopefully no one would question him in here. It might be harder to explain his presence.

He tried each door in turn, finding them all locked. The hallway ended in a small conclave, with an elevator and a door leading to a staircase. Obviously stairs would be the best option, but which way? Up or down? He considered the options. Holding cells would most likely be on a lower level, and if he took the stairs he could check out each level as he came to it. Opening the stairwell doorway he headed down, taking the stairs two at a time.

* * *

He could hear activity on the first floor down before he was even halfway there. A rifle range, no doubt. The sound of muffled gunfire was as familiar as the back of his hand. There was little chance that they'd locate holding cells by a rifle range -- too much chance of someone being hit by a stray bullet, or distracting a shooter at a vital time. He calculated the odds of Wren being on that floor as miniscule, and didn't even pause at the entrance, continuing on down into the bowels of the building.

How convenient. The next level was labeled "Holding and Processing." He ignored the part that advised only authorized personnel were to enter.

Summoning his best glower just in case someone was on the other side, he shouldered the door open and paused to survey the layout. As on the floor he'd just left, this level appeared to consist of a long hallway with numerous rooms branching off to either side. Starting at the closest room he started checking the rooms out one at a time. A large closet with various uniforms on the left. The next four doors bore the names of various officers, and were locked tight. He doubted there would be holding cells in any of those, so he moved on. The next room housed an impressive array of assault equipment and he paused long enough to liberate a couple of smoke grenades and a small pistol with a couple of clips of ammo. The familiar weight of the weaponry gave him some comfort.

On the seventh door, he hit pay dirt. The room contained six metal cages, with Wren occupying the one closest to the door.

"Snake? Is that really you? Oh thank God! Get me out of here!" Wren had never looked so happy to see him. Hell, if she wasn't confined in a metal cage in the center of the room, he bet she'd have thrown herself in his arms. Made a man feel wanted, having a woman look at him like that.

For the umpteenth time he wished she wasn't his buddy's kid sister. He was supposed to protect her from guys like himself, not take advantage of her. He shouldn't have touched her that night in the clearing, much less made mad, passionate love to her, but a guy could only take so much temptation. And Wren, well, temptation was putting it mildly. The sight of her in a pair of sweats taking out the garbage was enough to give him a hard-on. There was just something about her that made him go all caveman despite his best intentions. The woman was enough to drive a saint to drink!

Right now though, he needed to ignore his own needs and get her out of this place. They could sort out their relationship once she was safe.

They were in what appeared to be yet another office. Desks strewn with papers were placed haphazardly against the walls, while battered filing cabinets filled the spaces between them. A schedule with dates, times and names was tacked up on the wall to his left, while strange pictures that resembled something out of his high school science class decorated the entire wall behind Wren. Biology, maybe?

He quickly crossed to the cage, his gut clenching as he looked at the bruises on her legs. Once he got her out of here, he had a score to settle with these guys. No one laid a hand on his woman and got away with it, least of all a bunch of wanna-be soldiers.

He reached through the bars and ran his hand down the side of her face, pushing a strand of golden hair back behind her ear. "Yeah, it's me. The real question is what are you doing here?"

She avoided meeting his gaze. "I followed you. I thought you were going to see another woman, and it pissed me off. When you did your jump-the-fence thing, I walked up to the front entrance to see what kind of place this was and two men grabbed me." She shrugged. "And voilà. Here I am."

Snake shook his head. "Baby, you are so off - base. The last thing I want to be doing is stepping out with another woman."

She looked up, focusing those lovely hazel eyes on him. "Really? Because it seems like you spend most of your time thinking up ways to avoid me."

Snake let out a low groan. "Only because you deserve better than some washed-up mercenary." He grabbed the lock and gave it a hopeful tug. "Let's get you out of here. We can discuss us once you're safe. Any idea where the keys are?" He looked around, hoping for a handy key rack. No such luck. In the desk drawer maybe?

"We don't need keys."

"We don't?" He turned just in time to see Wren extract one of the pins she used to keep her hair in check. Taking the lock in her hand, she inserted the pin into the key slot and began to fiddle with it.

Snake felt his brow raise. "You can pick locks?"

A mischievous smile flitted across her face. "Among other things. I didn't grow up in a state-approved school."

He chuckled. "I can see that. Anything else I should know about you?"

Wren slanted him a cheeky look from beneath her long lashes and quoted his own words back to him. "We can discuss it once we're safely out of here."

He had to agree. "You're right. This is not the best place to be. I was checking out a nasty rumor I'd heard about this place. I had no intention of actually entering the buildings, but when I realized the woman being dragged through the main square wasn't a stranger I didn't have much choice." He captured her gaze. "Imagine my surprise."

Wren had the decency to look apologetic for a moment. "Okay. I probably should have stayed safely at home in my bed." She paused. "But it was lonely, and I'm really not good at doing what I should."

The lock fell open in her hand, and she held it up triumphantly. "There! I'm free to go."

Snake shook his head. "Sometimes doing what you should is what keeps you alive. Have you any idea how stupid it was to follow me here and get yourself captured?"

Wren sighed and rolled her eyes. "We're going to do this here? Of course I know it was dumb, almost as dumb as thinking you might actually give a flying fuck about me. So, either help me get out of here, or piss off and let me do it myself."

She certainly had regained her attitude in a hurry. "Yeah. Because you were doing a hell of a good job of it before I got here. Who's the eager youngster who volunteered to train you? You do know what he meant by 'train' don't you?"

Wren pushed past him without bothering to answer. Probably a good thing. Now that he knew she was okay, he was mad enough to… well… to do something. She could have got herself killed, or worse in this damn place.

Women!

Chapter Four

Damn Snake to hell anyways. It was his fault she'd gotten herself into this mess. If he'd quit giving off mixed signals and just tell her whether or not she had a chance with him then she wouldn't be skulking around in the shadows stalking him. First he ignored her, and then he let her seduce him into the most amazing night of sex she'd ever had and then he'd gone right back to ignoring her.

She got that he didn't like to talk, liked to play the strong and silent type. Really she did. But you can't treat a gal like she's the most amazing person on the face of the earth one day, and then ignore her like she's got some kind of interplanetary plague the next. It just wasn't fair!

"We're in a sub-basement of the main building."

She wasn't quite sure how he managed it, but Snake managed to insert himself between her and the door before she managed to open it. "We need to get to the stairs at the end of this corridor."

He obviously knew more about the layout than she did, so much as her pride wanted her to say screw you, she should probably let him take the lead. "How far to the stairwell?"

"About twenty yards. Most of the doors between here and there open into offices that looked deserted when I came past them."

She gave him a brittle smile. Well, she bared her teeth and that was about the best she could manage at the moment. "Let's hope they still are. Left or right?"

Snake frowned, a confused look on his face. Apparently his mind reading skills weren't any better than hers. She sighed. "Do we go left or right when we leave here?"

"Oh. Right." A ghost of a smile curved the corner of his lip. "We go right. The stairs are at the very end of the hall."

"Well then, let's get moving."

Snake opened his mouth to reply, but stopped. The ping of the elevator doors, followed by the sound of footsteps heading their way called for an immediate change of plans.

"Not yet!" Grabbing the lock, he threaded it back through the bars of the cage. "Quick, get back in here. Someone's coming."

Wren's brows shot skyward. "And you think it's a good idea to hang around and play with them?"

He shook his head, half of his attention on the sound of the approaching footsteps. "No, but if they see you still in the cage they won't suspect anything is out of the ordinary. Whatever you do, don't look at me."

* * *

She looked doubtful, but he didn't have time to reassure her. He looked around. His best bet was an alcove just to the side of the door. When the door swung open, the space would be blocked long enough to give him the element of surprise.

Locking his gaze on hers, he watched as she climbed back into the cage and set the lock to look as though it hadn't been tampered with. He noticed she didn't go quite as far as to actually relock it, not that he blamed her.

Grabbing a heavily weighted baton from the weapons rack, he slipped into the alcove. Turned out, it wasn't as big as it looked, and his shoulders scraped both sides of the space. He gave an exaggerated grimace, and was rewarded by a slight relaxing of the tension in Wren's face. Then the door burst open, and two burly thugs entered the room.

Wren actually winked at him before she took a deep breath and let out a bloodcurdling scream.

Good girl! The unexpected noise had the effect of focusing the thugs' attention on her, leaving him free to step out of his hiding spot and render them both unconscious with a couple of well-placed blows.

"That went well. Now can I get out of here?" Wren grinned saucily and flipped the lock on the cage. The door swung open and she stepped out, picking her way over the two bodies lying unmoving on the floor.

Snake snorted. "Could I stop you? That scream was brilliant. Let's just hope it didn't carry too far."

A worried frown creased her brow. "Do you think it did? It seemed like a good idea at the time."

It was his turn to grin. "Maybe, but in a place like this they must be used to the occasional woman's scream. Let's get moving before we find out for sure."

He eased open the door and stuck his head out into the corridor. He sensed her moving up behind him just before her unique scent filled his nostrils, flooding his senses with an all too familiar yearning. It took all of his willpower to ignore the heady invitation. Reaching back, he took her hand. "All clear. Let's go."

The corridor seemed ten times longer than it had on the way in. Snake walked on the balls of his feet, making as little sound as possible. He noticed Wren followed suit, keeping right behind him and matching his pace. His little bird was no stranger to perilous situations.

It looked like they were going to make it back to the stairs without being detected. Snake knew there had to be surveillance cameras mounted all over the place, but so long as they didn't do anything out of the ordinary they shouldn't trigger any alarms. In his experience the people who monitored the cameras had half their attention elsewhere.

He glanced up as the bank of elevators came into view. One of the three was in operation, and if the glowing numbers above it were to be believed, it was heading down their way.

Damn!

He did a quick mental calculation. They might just be able to get out of here. Tightening his grip on Wren's hand, he broke into a sprint.

The stairwell loomed closer.

The glowing numbers on the elevator continued their steady decline.

He burst through the metal door into the stairwell without slowing down, dragging a silent Wren behind him. The elevator let out a light ping, signaling the arrival of someone in the corridor they'd just vacated. If they were lucky whoever it was had come for some reason unconnected to Wren.

He didn't feel lucky today.

"What now?" Wren's voice sounded positively cheerful, but a quick glance told him she was faking it. Her eyes betrayed her fear.

"We get the hell out of here." He sure hoped his tone conveyed more assurance than he felt.

"I need to recheck the mess roster, and then we can work on the..." A strange voice trailed off into the distance on the far side of the metal stairwell door.

Wren looked up at him with visible relief. "They weren't coming for me."

Snake shook his head. "Not this time. Let's get moving before someone does."

"Sounds like a plan to me." She looked up at him expectantly, the tip of her tongue playing across her lips nervously.

* * *

By the time they reached the ground floor, he'd managed to get his libido under control. He paused at the exit door. "Okay, this is how we're going to play this. I lead the way. You walk behind me. Keep your head down and try not to do anything to attract attention."

Wren nodded. "Okay, but Snake?"

"Yes?"

"If we don't make it, I want you to know I appreciate you coming in after me. I shouldn't have been following you, and I shouldn't have let those idiots at the gate get their hands on me."

"We're going to make it." He wouldn't allow any other outcome. "Remember not to look up. All the women I've seen in this place are totally focused on the guy they're with. Now let's blow this joint!" Dropping her hand he pulled the door open and stepped out into enemy territory.

He knew Wren was right behind him, could sense her every move. He kept his stride steady, his steps deliberate. If they made it out the front door they stood a good chance of getting clear of this place, but if not he intended to fight with every dirty trick he'd learned over the years. No one was taking his woman from him.

No one.

They just needed to get to the end of the corridor undetected. Luckily most administrative personnel worked banker's hours, and the offices should be empty at this time of night.

One foot in front of the other, the only way to get home.

He slipped one hand behind his back and gave Wren an all-clear signal, but he didn't dare turn to reassure her. There would be video monitors in this part of the building and he had no way of telling how attentive the guards were. Fixing the end of the hallway with a steely gaze, he strode toward the main hallway.

Wren would keep up. He had faith in her ability to do what was necessary to gain her freedom. She'd survived as an orphan in a world that wasn't kind to orphans, and in an enclave where her worth was judged by her ability to fight. She wouldn't let him down now.

* * *

Wren watched the play of muscles across Snake's back. Tension showed in every movement, every step he took, but given the circumstances that wasn't a bad thing. She'd gotten herself into this mess and he'd stepped right in after her. She supposed she should feel guilty about that but some small part of her took hope in the fact that he'd put himself on the line to get her out of here. Surely that meant something.

If only she could figure him out. One moment, cold as ice and the next the best damn lover this side of the planet Mars. If they managed to get out of here she was going to pin him down one way or the other. Not knowing how he felt about her was driving her insane!

Snake slowed as they approached the end of the corridor and Wren followed suit, making sure to keep her eyes focused on the floor at his feet. They were entering the main foyer and the chances of running into someone who'd already seen her were at their highest here.

Her chest felt tight, her breathing difficult. If they were stopped, they'd have to fight their way out and they were drastically outnumbered. She had to restrain herself from crossing her fingers like some dumb little schoolgirl.

They were going to make it. She wouldn't accept any other outcome.

Snake started across the great hall, his stride long and confident. Wren followed suit. What was that old saying? Fake it till you make it? Snake seemed to have it down to a science.

Out of the corner of her eye, she saw one of the guards who'd originally brought her in, the older of the two. He had his back partially turned to her as he filled out some paperwork at one of the stations.

Please don't let him see me. Please don't let him see me. Please don't let him see me. She repeated the phrase over and over in her mind, as if saying it would somehow make it come true.

A group of younger men in sweats and T-shirts headed toward the main doors, cutting off her view of the guard, and she sent up a silent prayer of thanks to whatever god had answered her prayer.

They were two thirds of the way to the exit, and she wasn't sure she could take the tension much longer. Somehow, this felt worse than when they fought their way out of the enclave she'd been held captive in last year. There at least they'd had the pandemonium of mass chaos to cover their escape.

It seemed like a lifetime before Snake's hands were on the release bar of the door, and then, just like that, they were outside.

But they weren't out of danger yet. They still needed to get out of the compound.

Snake led her off to a set of stairs at the side of the building, keeping up the same pace he'd used inside the building. When they reached the bottom of the stairway he picked up the pace, breaking into a slow jog, as they ambled across the open space toward the tree line. She didn't dare say a word, keeping her head down and trying to use her peripheral vision to make sure no one was paying too much attention to them. It seemed like an eternity, but they finally entered the wooded area away from the prying eyes of any of the people in the compound.

Snake turned to gather her up in his arms and she melted against him, some of the tension draining out of her body.

Tears she hadn't known she was holding back threatened to spill, and she buried her face in the crook of his neck. She didn't deserve him, but after him sticking his neck out to save her dumb ass she began to hope that maybe, just maybe, he might feel the same way about her as she felt about him.

"We're not home free yet." His gruff voice sounded from somewhere above her head. "I'll feel a lot better when I have you on the far side of that rock wall."

Wren took a deep breath, and straightened her back. "Let's get going then. Can't have you losing it when we're this close to freedom." She didn't dare look up for fear he'd see how close she'd come to breaking down.

Snake captured her hand, and together they walked toward the high wall and safety.

* * *

"So what can you tell us?"

Wren was glad Snake was beside her, the focus of Kaeden's piercing stare.

"It's hard to say exactly what's going on in that place." Snake shook his head. "I didn't get a really good look at the operation, but it sounds like the Alliance has decided to try some bizarre breeding program involving soldiers and female conscripts. From what I gathered when they tried to acquire Wren, the females are not necessarily willing partners."

"Is it an offshoot of the lost children fiasco?"

Snake shrugged. "Hard to say. Maybe. There was some mention of enhancing the kids but to be honest, I was more focused on getting Wren out than gathering intel."

"We need to find out." Winter spoke up from her place beside Trace. "We can't let them do that again. We just can't."

"Don't worry." Kaeden glanced around the room. "We'll look into it and if it looks like a reboot of that program we'll take it down."

Saralyn stood up, stretching her arms over her head. "We don't have to go back in and risk anyone getting seen. As long as I know the address I can hack into their systems and see what's up."

"You can do that from here?" Snake sounded skeptical.

She nodded, a complacent smile curving the corner of her lips. "I can. You could have saved yourself all this trouble if you'd just asked me to take a peek for you. By tomorrow morning we'll know all about the Alliance's operations in that place and then we can decide what to do." She looked around the room before addressing Kaeden. "If it's okay with you, I'll go get started."

Kaeden grinned. "Fine with me. Save us a whole lot of legwork, and I can think of much better things to do with my evening than surveillance on an Alliance Facility."

"Me too." Snake dropped an arm around Wren's shoulder, deliberately staking his claim in front of his teammates.

Kaeden raised his brows. "Like that is it?"

Snake nodded. "Yup, it is."

"Well, make sure you take good care of her then." Kaeden glanced down at his own partner, Wren's big sister Dee. "I've grown fond of the brat since we were forced to go fetch her home."

"Brat?" Wren smiled sweetly. "I've been on my best behavior since I got here."

Snake rolled his eyes. "And that's why I had to bust you out of an Alliance enclave tonight?"

She shrugged. "That was your bad. If you'd told me where you were going I wouldn't have had to follow you."

Kaeden laughed. "You might as well give up now, Snake. You know you're never going to get the last word." He stood up. "Okay, guys. Until Saralyn has a chance to see what she can dig up, this meeting is over. Go get some sleep."

* * *

The door closed with a deliberate thud, and Snake turned to face her, already shedding his clothing. Wren followed his example, the clothing she wore nothing more than a barrier between her and the man she'd loved since the first time he'd rescued her. She really had to stop making a habit of getting kidnapped!

Dropping the final piece of clothing to the floor, she kicked it aside. It had taken more self-control than she'd thought she possessed to wait until they were done explaining the events of the evening to his teammates before retreating to Snake's room.

Desire spiraled through her, robbing her of breath. He looked so damn sexy standing in the shadows of the room, his naked body outlined by the moonlight flooding through the window. He held out his hand in silent invitation, and she crossed to his side.

His hands closed over her shoulders, gently pulling her in closer. She could feel the leashed tension in his touch.

"Are you sure?" The husky rasp of his voice had a sensual quality to it, sending shivers of lust curling across the surface of her skin. "Once I take you this time there's no going back. I let you go once, and I don't think I can do that again. I know you'd be better off with someone else, but I'm just not that strong. You'll be mine. Forever."

Wren let a sliver of a smile ghost across her lips. The man had no idea how sexy he looked, standing there trying to give her a choice. She'd already made it, long ago. Snake was everything she'd ever wanted in a man. Not just a lover, he was solid, dependable and decent.

"I'm already yours." She wound her arms around his neck, her eyes fluttering closed as she covered his lips with hers for an endlessly delightful moment. "And I have no intention of ever letting you go, so you might as well get used to it. You're doomed to spend the rest of your life trying to please me."

"Well then." His hands slid from her back down to cup her ass and press her against him. "I guess I'd better get started."

Wren pretended to pout. "I guess you'd better, and you better be sure to make it good."

"Is that a challenge?" A hint of laughter infected Snake's voice.

Wren slanted him a look from beneath her lashes. "What do you think?"

"Sounded like an order." Snake ran a finger down her cheek. "One I'm more than happy to follow."

His finger resting beneath her chin, Snake lowered his head, feathering a kiss across her lips. Wren closed her eyes, savored the feel of his lips on hers while his naked body pressed against her.

He worshipped her with his mouth, there was no other way to describe it. She felt warm and protected, knowing beyond a shadow of a doubt that this man would go to the ends of the known universe and beyond for her. He'd followed her into that hell hole and brought her out safe and sound. Sappy as it sounded, he was her hero.

Snake's mouth moved to her neck, raining little kisses all the way down to her shoulder as he ran his hands down her side and lifted her up, his hands cradling her butt. Wren wrapped her legs around his waist, locking her heels behind his back to hold herself in place.

"I love you so much, it almost hurts." Snake buried his head in the crook of her shoulder, the words muffled against her skin. Wren could feel the tip of his cock against her and wriggled her butt, positioning herself directly above it.

Snake lifted his head to stare directly into her eyes. She could see the hot desire burning in their depths, but there was something else too. Something that made her feel precious and important. Loved. She felt loved.

Snake lowered her onto his cock, slowly, one delicious inch at a time. She whimpered softly as need exploded through her. Darts of liquid fire crawled across the surface of her skin, provoking her to dig her fingernails into Snake's back as she tried to make him move faster, tried to impale herself on his deliciously stiff cock.

"Not so fast, love. I want you to feel every single moment. I want you to know beyond a shadow of a doubt that you are mine." He kept his gaze locked on her as he began to move in and out, going just a little deeper with each thrust until, finally, after what felt like an eternity, she felt his balls snug up against her ass cheeks.

She knew she should reply, should tell him how much she loved him. She needed him to know that she would always be his, that she looked forward to the day when she would hold a child of theirs in her arms. She wanted to tell him so much, but her body was too busy to allow her mind the kind of concentration needed to form coherent sentences.

She settled for a kiss.

Locking her arms around his neck Wren poured all of her feelings into one hot, fiery kiss. She devoured him with that kiss, taking in every bit of his being and making it hers. Snake kissed her back while he continued to move her up and down on his rigid shaft. Their bodies merged, becoming one in a dance as old as the universe.

The orgasm took them both together, pouring over them like a tsunami of pleasure so intense it almost hurt. They clung to each other as wave after wave of aftershocks rocked their world.

Finally, the intensity lessened. Snake took two staggering steps and they collapsed together on his bed. They clung to each other, neither willing to let the moment come to an end. Their breath came in long gasps, and their hearts were still racing. Wren opened her eyes, drinking in the sight of her man lying beside her. Her man. Her love. Her life.

They were together and nothing else mattered.

Anne Kane

Anne Kane lives in the beautiful Okanagan Valley with a bouncy little rescue dog whose breed defies description and an Aussie Shepherd who's too smart for her own good. Anne likes to write spicy stories with sassy heroines and protective, sexy male heroes who love those women. Her stories all have one thing in common: a happily ever after ending.

Her hobbies, when she's not playing with the characters in her head, include kayaking, hiking, swimming, playing guitar, and spoiling the grandkids.

Anne at Changeling: changelingpress.com/anne-kane-a-116

Changeling Press E-Books

More Sci-Fi, Fantasy, Paranormal, and BDSM adventures available in e-book format for immediate download at ChangelingPress.com -- Werewolves, Vampires, Dragons, Shapeshifters and more -- Erotic Tales from the edge of your imagination.

What are E-Books?

E-books, or electronic books, are books designed to be read in digital format -- on your desktop or laptop computer, notebook, tablet, Smart Phone, or any electronic e-book reader.

Where can I get Changeling Press E-Books?

Changeling Press e-books are available at ChangelingPress.com, Amazon, Apple Books, Barnes & Noble, and Kobo/Walmart.

Changeling Press, LLC

ChangelingPress.com